4-6

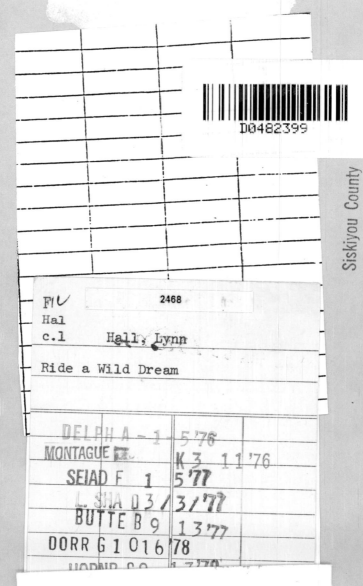

RIDE A WILD DREAM

RIDE A WILD DREAM

Lynn Hall

Illustrated by GEORGE ROTH

FOLLETT PUBLISHING COMPANY
Chicago

SBN 695-87737-2 Trade binding
SBN 695-47737-4 Titan binding

Library of Congress Catalog Card Number: 69-15961

Fourth Printing I

FOR MY MOTHER AND FATHER

Except for the blue-white light from the television screen, the living room was dark, even darker than the front yard beyond the window. Although there was no moon, the snow on the ground and in the air picked up the glow of the barn light around the corner of the house and reflected its whiteness.

Hunched on the cedar chest that doubled as a window seat, Jon could feel the cold coming in around the window. He shifted his seat bones to a more comfortable position and flexed his feet. One leg was asleep.

"Aren't those guys ever coming home?" he muttered. "The games are always over by nine."

"You say something?" Aunt Jess called from the kitchen.

"No, nothing. What time is it?"

"Nine-thirty. They'll be home pretty soon. I expect this snow's slowed them down some."

For an instant, he thought he saw headlights, but it was only the porch light going on at Whites' house across the road and a quarter-mile to the south. Again, there was nothing to see but the trees that filled the long slope of the front yard, stark black shapes against the bluish snow. He re-focused his eyes on the reflections of the television screen in the window glass—a double reflection, really, one on the inside and one on the storm window. He sighed.

"Ouch, you dumb cat!" Two needles of pain touched his stomach as Ben, who was curled uncomfortably in the sharp angle of his lap, stretched and unsheathed his claws. One slitted eye opened, then closed again as Jon's finger found his chin. The cat craned his neck and began to purr.

From the dining room behind him, Jon could hear his father sighing heavily, stirring through the papers on his desk, muttering.

"Next year I'm hiring a tax man, Jess, I swear. Lot of nonsense. Now I can't find that depreciation table. . . ."

Heck, they don't even care, Jon thought with irritation. They're not the least bit interested in whether

8

Elton and Ernie ever get home. This could be just any old night as far as they're . . .

A spot of light appeared over the rise in the road near Whites' place.

"Here they come," he yelled. Ben leaped to the floor.

The headlights grew nearer, slowed for the turn into the lane, then suddenly swayed and veered up toward the sky. They were still for a few moments. Then they disappeared.

"They went in the ditch by the mailbox," he announced. Dad rose grumbling from his desk. Aunt Jess went out onto the back porch to look. "It's okay," Jon said. "I can see them both walking."

Through the trees he could make out the canted shape of the car and the forms of his brothers plodding, leaning into the wind. A few yards up the lane they stopped abruptly, stood looking down, then stooped to the ground. When they straightened up, it seemed to Jon that each of them was holding something, but the light was tricky, and he couldn't be sure.

"I hope that wasn't my present they just dropped in the snow," he muttered.

He unfolded himself from the cedar chest and went through the long dark living room, around the semi-lighted dining room behind Dad's hunched shape, and into the bright warmth of the kitchen. Aunt Jess was just closing the cupboard door on the cake. Anticipation shivered through his stomach. Unless something went horribly wrong, the beginning of the end of the dreaming would come now.

There was shuffling on the back porch, and then the kitchen was filled with Elton and Ernie and the cold air they brought in with them. Through the foot-stamping, the loud breathing of coming into a warm kitchen from a cold night, and the exchanges of greetings, Aunt Jess said, "Well, how was the game, and how was the road coming home? Did you go to the Bluebird and get a good supper, or just . . . Good night! What've you got under those jackets!"

The room was silent. Jon's eyes moved quickly between his brothers' faces, while his thumbnail dug into a bubble of paint on the chair in front of him.

Ernie, suppressing a grin, passed the responsibility to Elton with a glance. Jon tried to read Elton's face. It said either guilt or sheepishness or discomfort at being the center of attention, or possibly pleasure. Jon was never sure with Elton.

"Here. Happy birthday." Elton's hand plunged into his jacket and came out holding a spiky-furred white pup. Jon stared, nonplussed for a moment.

Then Ernie was holding out a second pup. "And here's the other half. We didn't want to break up the set."

Grinning, Jon took a pup into each hand and moved automatically to the warmth of the register. He held the shivering scraps close to his ribs as he squatted atop the register. Almost instantly their trembling slackened.

Dad and Aunt Jess asked together, "Where on earth did you get those?"

Aunt Jess added, "Was that what you were picking up out there in the lane? Somebody dumped strays on a night like this?"

There was no answer. Jon looked up in time to see Ernie glance uneasily from him to Aunt Jess.

"They're Elton's birthday present to Jon, and it's not polite to ask. . . . I wonder what we did with the screen?"

With an air of relief, Elton pounded down the basement stairs. "I know where it is. I'll get it."

"Well." Aunt Jess's tone said the subject was closed. She sat down at the table and patted her aproned lap. "Bring them here. I'll hold them while you get some papers. And you better put some milk on to warm. Poor little rats."

Dad bent over the pups for a quick look, said they looked to him like they had some collie in them, and went back to his desk in the dining room. From the stack of newspapers on the back porch, Jon got a bundle of *Des Moines Sunday Registers* and laid a thick carpet of them in the alcove between the stove and the jut of wall by the basement stairs. As he got the milk carton from the refrigerator, Elton came up from the basement, carrying the screen. It was half of an old screen door, cut to fit exactly across the alcove. It had fenced in puppies before, and an occasional runt pig, and once a gosling.

When the pups had been set on the newspapers and had christened them appropriately, Jon was able to get a good look at them. They did seem to be of the collie family, about two months old, he guessed. Both were nearly solid white. One had a brown face and a brown spot on his rump; the other had brown ears only. They wagged slowly around the enclosure, sniffing the paper and looking up frequently with bright black eyes.

"They look kind of potbellied, don't they," Elton mused. "Probably wormy."

When the pups had been given the pan of warm milk and some hamburger, Aunt Jess called to Dad, "Come on, John. Time for you-know-what. You boys go wash the dog off your hands. Just because the whole room smells of wet dog, the food doesn't have to taste like it, too."

According to family custom, the refreshments ritual was disposed of before the main event, the presents. There was the standard chocolate cake with seven-minute icing—the only kind Aunt Jess ever made —with "Happy Birthday, Jon" and a big "12" on top; ice cream and whipped hot chocolate with marshmallows were side features.

Jon worked through his cake warily. Aunt Jess was bad about egg shells.

Elton forgot to buy me a present, he thought. Ernie probably didn't forget, but Elton sure did. Or else he just didn't want to spend the money. He wouldn't have dared to forget Dad's birthday, or Aunt Jess's. Oh well, the dogs are better than anything he would have bought me, so why should I give a darn. Besides, that isn't the important thing, anyhow.

". . . made nine baskets," Elton was boasting, "and one of them was from way out in the middle of the floor."

"Thanks to some A-number-one defensive play and a lot of dumb luck," Ernie added.

Aunt Jess rose to get the coffeepot. "I guess we'll have to go in and see a game one of these times, John, as long as we got the two stars in the family. More coffee?"

Dad held out his cup.

Jon fought back his impatience as Aunt Jess moved around the table in slow motion, refilling her coffee cup and the three hot chocolate mugs, adding fresh marshmallows, removing cake plates and ice cream bowls.

What if Dad decides not to for me? he thought, his stomach on edge. Just because he did for Elton and Ernie doesn't automatically mean he will for me. There're lots of things they got to do younger than I did. They were both . . .

Aunt Jess was setting a small stack of packages on the table in front of him. "Happy twelfth birthday."

This is it. This is it, Jon breathed.

He opened the first one. The sweater Aunt Jess had been knitting since Christmas—he'd known about that. Then there was a large book, *The Horseman's Encyclopedia.* The card was signed "from Ernie and Elton," but the "and Elton" was in different ink. Good old Ernie. He leafed through the volume, tantalized, then set it aside.

Two envelopes lay on the table. The first was a card and ten dollars from Grandma and Grandpa McBride. The second said simply "Jon" in Dad's handwriting. As he picked it up, the tension slipped out of him. Here it was.

Inside was a piece of lined paper from the small notebook Dad carried in his shirt pocket. It read, "This entitles Jonathon McBride to one gilt sow, of his choice, and free board and keep for her for one year. All money earned from pigs from this sow belongs to him, to do with as he sees fit. John McBride."

Dad cleared his throat and scraped back his chair. "Now that don't give you the right to spend that money foolishly, Jon. If you're smart, you'll keep back all the female shoats for breeding, like the other boys did, and just sell off the males. That money can help with your school clothes and the like."

Except for the soft snoring of one of the pups and the wind outside, the kitchen was still. Very carefully, still looking down at the notepaper, Jon said, "Um, Dad, if I do like you said and keep back all the females, and if there's enough males in her first litter to buy what I need for school and have some left over —to buy a horse, can I? If I pay you back out of my own money for the winter feed, and of course do all the work of taking care of it myself, and all that?" He was afraid to stop talking, afraid of what Dad might say.

Elton and Ernie exchanged "I told you so" glances. Aunt Jess watched her brother as he shook out a cigarette and ignited a match with a flick of his thumb. Jon watched him, too, trying frantically to read the familiar red-leather face.

Dad's forehead rose in wrinkles that ended abruptly where the hairline used to be. "Horse, huh?" He pulled on his cigarette, then knocked the ash off into his cupped palm. "Oh, the other boys wasted theirs on cars. I don't suppose it's any different if you waste yours on horses. But I'll tell you one thing— there's going to be a limit on how *much* of that money you spend on any horse. And, there's going to be no letting your work slide, and no coming to me if it turns out you bought yourself a dud. Understand?"

Jon's head nodded once, in slow motion. He was floating through the vacuum of relief. We're in the bag now, horse. We're home free. . . .

When Jon had gone up to his room and the twins were watching the late movie in the living room, Jess refilled the two coffee cups and lowered herself into her chair. She twisted around to look at the pups, who were curled into tight-linked circles. They were thoroughly warm and dry now and seemed to be smiling in their sleep.

"That was awful of Elton to forget Jonnie's birthday." She spoke quietly, aware of the register overhead that carried sounds, as well as heat, to Jon's room.

John McBride wrapped his hand around his coffee cup and remained silent.

"I hope he gets a gentle one," she said after a while. "He's such a slight boy. It sure doesn't seem like he could be twelve already. And horses can be awful unpredictable."

John snorted lightly. "He'll be okay. When Whites had their horses, the twins rode like little Indians, and they were younger than Jon."

"Not so loud. That was the twins. Jonnie's cut from a different bolt of goods, and it's not fair to judge them the same. Jon's his mother's boy."

Her words hung in the silent kitchen for a moment before he answered. His voice was low and harsh. "*None* of them are her boys! She didn't want them, and she didn't want . . ." His jaw bulged for an instant; then he went on more calmly. "Jon just seems like her because he's light-complected like her, but don't you worry about that boy. He's a McBride.

"Besides, it'll be the better part of a year till he's got that hog money. Chances are he'll have forgotten all about a horse by that time. Maybe he'll get him an old car to fix up, like Elton did. And now he's got

16

those dogs to make pets out of. Let's go see what the late show is."

He moved heavily through the dining room and stood for a moment in the arched doorway of the living room. The blue glow from the television outlined the identical faces and man-sized bodies of his eldest sons, touched the crisp black of their hair—just like his own had been. His heart ached with pride at their bigness, their rough grace, their good minds and smooth, strong faces. He thought of Jon upstairs and wished with all his soul he could love his third son as much.

2

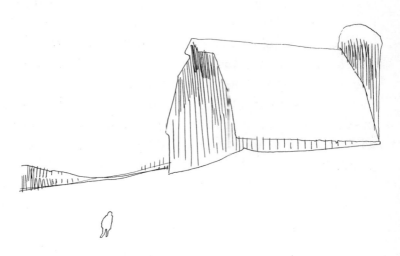

During breakfast, the kitchen radio announced that there would be no school today in the New Hope Consolidated Schools due to heavy snow and excessive drifting; all county roads should be cleared by afternoon. The three boys celebrated by eating a big, leisurely breakfast in their pajamas.

The pups were ready for the new day. They rolled and tumbled with each other. They polished the pan of milk Jon set down for them and then cleaned up the egg and bacon and toast-corner scraps from the table. They stood on unsteady hind legs and scratched at the screen and showed round pink bellies.

They followed the movements and voices of everyone at the table, especially Jon.

"What are you going to name them?" Ernie asked.

Jon looked down at the four bright black eyes, the two black noses that were pointed at him through the screen. "Well, since they're a male and a female, and since they're sort of like a team, you might say, I think I'll name them Sade and Sam."

Aunt Jess and Dad exchanged quick glances, remembering how Jon had made himself sick from crying six years ago, when the old team of workhorses died within a day of each other. Sade and Sam had been well past twenty then. They hadn't worked for years, except for the very light job of carrying small boys around the pasture and up the lane on their broad, high backs. The whole family, even Dad, had put in a bad day when the truck from the rendering plant came and took the mountainous brown bodies away. Jon had been unconsolable.

Dad scraped back his chair. "Well, you boys better get dressed. We'll plow out the lane and see what we can do about getting the car out of the ditch."

While the twins and Dad fixed the snow blade to the tractor, Jon trudged in the opposite direction toward the barn. It was a silent, crystal morning, with waves of unbroken snow stretching away from the house, across the backyard and the broad flat area around which the outbuildings were arranged in a casual circle. He stopped for a minute, hating to be the one to mar the snow. It sparkled so brightly in the sun that he had to squint his eyes. Ahead and to his right loomed the barn, its whiteness almost dingy against the snow.

"This time next year I'll be coming out here in the mornings to feed my horse," he mused as he opened the barn door.

Inside, it was dark gray and colder than outdoors. As soon as his eyes adjusted to the dimness, he found the feed bucket and went into the small room where the chicken feed was stored. A large yellow and white cat with half of his tail missing was curled on top of the half-full grain sack.

"Morning, Ben. Get down now."

The cat stretched fore and aft, yawned, and thudded to the floor. He collected his morning chin-scratching from Jon; it was unsatisfactory because Jon was wearing heavy gloves. Disgruntled, he stalked out into the main barn. Jon followed with the bucket of feed.

The main part of the barn was a vast dust-covered arena with a few tie stalls for horses along the far wall, a double row of milk-cow stanchions down the middle, and a maze of small rooms and corners and half-walled pens here and there on either side. The stanchions had been empty for years, but the names could still be seen, painted on the metal bars—Belle, Daisy, Gretchen. The horse stalls were filled with stacks of feed bags, bundles of baling twine, bits of machinery, oil drums, gray-brown miscellany.

Suddenly aware that his toes were cold, he left the barn and plodded across the expanse of snow to the brooder house. He ducked through the low door and said, "Okay, you guys, come and get it." The air in the tiny building was filled with cackles and fluttering, feathers and flakes of chicken droppings, as the dozen or so small white hens crowded around the tiny trough on the floor. They jostled and pecked just as though there weren't plenty of room and plenty of cracked corn to go around. He poured his load of gold evenly down the length of the trough, then checked the warming unit in the water fountain.

As he started back to the barn with the empty bucket, he passed Ernie on his way to the hog barn. "Wait a minute, I'll go with you." Looking down the lane, he could see that Elton and Dad had plowed to the road and were bent over the front of Elton's car with the tow chain.

He tossed the bucket inside the barn and ran to catch up with Ernie. The hog barn was long and low and newer than the main barn; it had concrete floors and rows of low-walled pens, divided by pipe barriers. The cold from the concrete came through Jon's galoshes and found his toes.

While Ernie turned on the electric augers that started the feed on its way to the troughs, Jon went through the barn to the small lot behind it, where the year-old gilt sows were. He'd been watching them for weeks, studying conformation. disposition, eagerness in eating. There was one he liked in particular, but it was a big decision.

He stepped up onto the fence and sought her out. The white curve of her back rose a good three inches above the others. She was long-bodied and deep through the heart, and her small eyes were hidden by the coy flaps of her ears. With caution born of experience, Jon slid over the fence and made his way toward her. When she felt his hand on her shoulder, she peered around at him for a moment, then looked away. The leather-like skin showed pink through her sparse white bristle. The line of her back was nearly as high as his waist.

Ernie called from the barn door, "Got your sow picked out?" He came over the fence.

"Yeah, I think so. This one here."

Ernie pursed his lips and looked her over, ready to offer criticism of Jon's choice, but unable to think of any. "Is this one of the ones that was bred last week?"

"Yes, so she'll be among the first batch to farrow in May. I looked her up in the record book, and she came from a litter of twelve, so I figured she should be a good producer." He waited for Ernie to compliment him on his choice.

"I suppose you're going to name her."

Jon said with dignity, "Well, of course not."

You could get away with naming dogs or horses or cats without getting teased, but you didn't name the livestock. When Ernie was safely out of earshot, he murmured, "But just between you and me, I think I'll call you Fortune, because that's what you're going to bring me, okay?" The sow grunted and lumbered away.

Long before lunchtime the whole family was back in the house, silently reveling in its warmth and in the fact that no one had to go out again. "Times like these," Aunt Jess said, as she gazed out the kitchen window, "I'm glad we don't have dairy cows or anything like that that needs a lot of choring in the winter."

"What do you care?" Dad said. "You're not the one that has to do it." She ignored him and started lunch.

The afternoon was long and lazy. Aunt Jess settled with her knitting and the Channel Four Afternoon Movie in the living room. Dad went back to his desk and the income tax forms. Elton went out to work on his car—it was his and Ernie's jointly, but Elton was the one who loved it. Ernie went upstairs and shut himself in his bedroom, which doubled as his ham radio shack. The cardboard sign on the door said, "Ernie McBride, KØ RAV, New Hope, Iowa. STAY OUT."

Jon spent the afternoon on the kitchen floor with the pups. He moved the screen from the pen to the dining room doorway, so they could have the run of the kitchen without endangering the carpet. Silly with freedom, the pups scrambled and bounced among chair and table legs, fought for the best position on Jon's lap, and wrestled with each other until they were exhausted. Then Sam fell asleep in the square of sunlight in front of the sink, and Sade clawed her way up to Jon's chest for her nap.

He slid a little lower on the floor and wrapped his arms around the sleeping white ball. Over the music of the television movie, he could hear the static of the ham radio upstairs, and Ernie's voice in loud conversation with one of his radio friends. Oddly, the ham set didn't irritate Jon today as it usually did. So Ernie had his own little world. So what? *He* had the promise of a horse. And of course the pups.

3

Within a week, the pups had perfected the art of climbing over their screen and had won themselves, perforce, the run of the house. It took them no time at all to learn to follow Jon up the stairs to the bedrooms, even though they were too timid to try going down the long, steep flight of steps.

Sam was the adventurer. He was constantly crying to be rescued from behind the furnace, atop the attic stairs, among shoe boxes in Elton's closet, and from behind the toilet where he periodically got himself wedged.

Sade was altogether different. She attached herself to Jon exclusively from the first day. While he was in school, she contented herself with Aunt Jess, but by midafternoon of even the coldest days, she was stationed beside the mailbox at the end of the lane where the school bus unloaded. She lay on his bed and watched with adoring eyes while he changed clothes. She followed him from main barn to chicken house to hog barn. She slept under his chair while he did his homework, and shoved her way into the bathroom with him if he absentmindedly started to close the door in her face. At night, against Aunt Jess's better judgment, Sade slept on Jon's bed, crowding his legs to one side.

On a soggy afternoon in late March, as the last of the snow was disappearing, Jon saw something lying beside the lane as he walked from the school bus. He detoured over to it and nudged it with the toe of his shoe.

It was the partly decomposed body of a puppy. Sade came close and sniffed with interest. What remained of the pelt was woolly brown, with white paws and chest. The pup was about the size Sade and Sam had been when the twins found them. Something, probably one of the cats, had been at it.

Jon's stomach churned. His arms tightened around his notebooks. "Come on, Sadie. Race ya." He ran the length of the lane at top speed and then a little faster, but there was no joy in his running. The brown carcass back in the lane was a grisly proof of what he already knew. Sade and Sam had provided Elton with a convenient, zero-hour rescue from the embarrassment of having forgotten Jon's birthday.

Silly thing to carry a grudge about all this time, he told himself. But the hurt stayed with him as he crossed the side yard and went into the kitchen. Aunt Jess was working at the sink.

"No Sam yet?" Jon dumped his books on the counter and peered into the cookie jar.

"The chocolate chips are all gone, but there's a box of fig bars in the cupboard if you want some. No, he hasn't come back yet. He's never stayed away this long before."

He carried the box of cookies with him as he moved from window to window around the kitchen. He stared long and carefully at the outbuildings, the fields, the strip of timbered pasture, but he knew he would see no white collie pup. Sam was gone for good this time. He'd been missing two nights and two days now, and he'd never stayed away more than a night at a time on any of his previous trips to wherever it was that he went.

"Maybe he just didn't like living on a farm," he said. Like Mom . . .

Sade pressed against him, her long torso moving in whiplash action against the swish of her tail. Her insistence roused him from his thoughts, and he went back to the job of opening the cookie box.

When he had gotten his fig bars and gone upstairs to change, Jess set down the head of lettuce she'd been tearing at, wiped her hands on her apron, and moved automatically around her kitchen, dumping the rest of the cookies into the jar and crumpling their box into the wastebasket, putting Jon's books out of the way in the dining room.

Jonnie doesn't seem very worried about Sam, she thought. Oh well, Sade's the one that's the pet, anyhow, and we really don't need two dogs. Maybe it's just as well.

She reached for the head of lettuce again, but a glance at the clock stopped her She sat down at the table instead, her hands in her lap. Only four-thirty. No need to start supper for another hour yet. An hour.

Her mind ranged over the possibilities. Nothing on television worth looking at, nothing in the kitchen that really needed doing. She heaved a mighty sigh of boredom. Spring fever, she chided herself. But the vague restlessness that came over her in odd moments didn't restrict itself to spring anymore, as it had when the boys were younger and there was always work to be done. It had grown a little more evident after John bought her the clothes dryer last year, and the dishwasher the year before when the corn crop had been so good. Now she had a little less work to do, a little more time to wonder if she'd done right, taking on the job of raising John's family instead of holding out for a husband and sons of her own.

She smiled wryly. Hah. I probably never would have caught a man anyhow, and if I had, chances are I wouldn't have gotten any more appreciation from a family of my own than I do from this one. She heaved herself up from the table and went back to work tearing at the lettuce.

For the next few weeks, the field work took precedence over everything else. Because Dad was in the fields at sunup, Jon and the twins got up early, too, and often put in an hour or so of plowing or discing before it was time to change for school.

In the afternoons until dark, and all day on weekends, Jon and the twins assumed tractor duty. All three of the tractors were going every daylight hour, except when one of them was down for repairs. The four men—Jon was considered a man during this season—spelled each other at eating and doing the necessary daily work of caring for the hogs and chickens.

Most of the time Jon was assigned the John Deere, because Dad judged it the safest of the three tractors. The plowing was endless, monotonous work, and he loved it, especially the first trip around a field that hadn't been worked since last fall. The gray-brown crusty earth in front of the old John Deere turned beneath the blades into rich moist crumbly black. The sight of it moved Jon in a way he didn't understand. He felt as if he and the old Deere were a team. He knew intimately every bolt and screw, every fleck of rust on the long green snout that stretched ahead of him. Each gear, each mud-crusted pedal, each toggle and lever, were a part of him. The Deere's roar and throb and unplumbed power became his.

This is how it'll feel on my horse, too, he thought. Only I can feel it any time I want to, not just at plowing time. I'll be up there on that high back, with all that power under me, and I'll be bigger than them. He imagined himself riding high above Elton and Ernie, smoothly controlling the dancing brute of a horse beneath him.

He resented school mornings, when he was reduced again to the size of a seventh grader.

Around the first of May, Dad and one of his brothers, who was semi-retired from his implement dealership, drove down to Missouri in the stock trucks, and bought calves to be fattened for fall butchering. They were gone three days, during which Elton and Ernie stayed home from school to plant the corn. Those mornings, as he waited for the school bus with Sade, Jon watched his brothers roaring slowly across the flat stretch of the cornfields. In his sport shirt and neat school slacks, he felt insignificant.

Dad and Uncle Jim drove in late Thursday evening, stiff and red-eyed from the twelve-hour drive. As the first truck was backed up against the loading chute beside the barn, Jon and Aunt Jess and the twins came from the house to greet the men and see the new calves.

Down the chute came the young steers, one by one, their wide brown eyes taking in the barn lot with nervous curiosity. They were herefords and hereford-angus crosses, not quite full grown, shaggy with their winter coats and crusted with dust. They milled about uneasily, their legs shaky after the long hours in the truck.

Between Jon and Aunt Jess, Sade sat and watched the cattle with growing interest. She hooked her chin over the middle board of the fence and followed each debarking calf with bright, hungry eyes. Her tail gathered momentum with every calf until it was slap-slopping against Jon's leg and Aunt Jess's.

After the rest of the family had gone up to the house for coffee, Jon ducked through the fence for a closer look. Every batch of calves on previous summers had included at least one character, one calf who followed the boys to get his neck scratched. Jon could never resist making pets of them and, when Dad was safely out of sight, riding them.

He moved slowly among the animals whose white faces seemed to stand out from their black or red bodies in the near-dark. They tensed and watched him through incredibly long white eyelashes.

Then Sade was moving past him toward the nearest calf. She trotted confidently and circled the calf so smoothly that the animal held his ground and stared at her, unruffled. Around the lot she went, flowing among the calves, touching an outstretched nose here and there, and moving on. Jon watched, fascinated. Finally she completed her tour and came back to him, wagging.

He smiled. "Hey there, pup, you going to be a cattle dog?"

On a Saturday afternoon late in May, Jon's sow began showing the restlessness he'd been waiting for. Heart pounding, he secured the gate on the farrowing pen she'd been wandering in and out of for a week, and then went to get more bedding. When Aunt Jess called supper, he yelled back from the barn door, "I can't come. Fortune's getting ready to farrow!"

Aunt Jess turned to Ernie, who was just coming up the back steps. "What did he say? Sounded like something about a fortune."

Ernie laughed. "I think that's what he named his sow, the little nut. I'll take his supper down to him if you want."

When Jon finished spreading the floor of the pen with oat straw, twice as thick as he would have for any other sow, he lowered himself to the floor against the wall to wait. But the sow glared out at him from beneath her flapping ears and moved away when he came near her. So, sighing, he climbed out of the pen and settled on a straw bale across the aisle.

Ernie brought his supper to him, and a book to read. Aunt Jess came later to take the dishes back and bring him a warmer jacket. Then they left him alone.

The sow lay down, got up, rooted the straw aside, wove back and forth across the pen.

"Please, old girl. A big litter, with lots of males. Three at the very, very least. I promise we won't butcher you for a couple more years yet, okay?"

At last, around midnight, she lay down again and got to business. Jon rose and went into the pen. Suddenly he felt queasy.

"After all the farrowing you've seen, you dummy?" His own voice in the silence of the barn made him jumpy.

The pigs were coming then. He squatted and began to dry each newborn, setting it gently at a nipple when he was through. Female . . . female . . . male . . . female . . . At length, it was all over. He sat back in the straw, exhausted and smiling. Five females, six males.

His horse was guaranteed.

If only they all lived . . . Sickened by the weight of this new worry, he got the side cutters and began the ticklish job of nipping the points of the babies' teeth, so they couldn't hurt each other or the sow.

His worried mind raced. There'll be shots later and then castrating and watching out for chills. He looked down at the newborn pigs and wondered how they—and he—were ever going to make it through the next few weeks.

4

In the middle of June, the planting was finished, and Jon and the green tractor began the endless job of cultivating the main cornfield. It was a long flat eighty acres, bordered on one side by the road and on the other by the lane that led from the barn lot to the pasture.

By six every morning, Jon was guiding the Deere down rows of corn shoots just inches high. Often, during the first hour or so, while the sky was still a soft gray-blue and the sun barely high enough to make shadows, he felt an intense poignancy, a beautiful sort of sadness because something was slipping away from him; he didn't know what. Then the sun would touch the dew-drenched rows ahead of him and set them to sparkling, and Cal White's tractor would appear in the field across the road, or maybe Dad's in the soybean field just east of the lane, and the feeling would go away.

Driving south, away from the house, he set his sights on the deep-green clumpy strip of timber along the creek in the pasture. Coming back, he aimed at the house, with its backdrop of windbreak pines and its long oak-studded front yard that protected it from the dust of the road and the eyes of people going by.

The house was seventy-four years old, square and white, with intricate wooden curlicues in the peaks of the roof, a large rail-enclosed front porch, and high, narrow windows. The angles of the house were softened by lilacs and snowball bushes. It had been designed and built by John McBride's grandfather to replace a very small three-room house that had, in turn, replaced the original log house. When Jon thought about it at all, the house suited him, and he was glad his roots went back so many generations. The thought was comforting sometimes, until he began thinking about how much more the place seemed to belong to everyone else in the family than it did to him. After all, he was just the little brother, third in line of inheritance, the oddball who didn't pull his share. When he thought of that, whatever job he was doing took on a little added weight.

Each morning, before he backed the Deere out

of the machine shed, Jon let the calves out of the barn lot and followed them down the lane to the pasture. They needed no urging after the first few mornings. They knew what was at the end of the lane. But Sade delighted in herding them anyway. In the evenings, she went with him to drive them back again for the night. Bringing the calves in each night was a procedure that Elton and Dad argued about from time to time. Elton said it was silly, but Dad insisted that a good stockman looked over his stock regularly, saw that they were gaining as they should be and not getting wire cuts or open sores that invited grubs.

After the first few days, Sade took over the tedious job of searching out the forty-odd young steers and starting them down the lane to their nightly prison, while Jon waited astride the gate. The pasture was nearly a hundred acres, most of it hilly, with wooded ravines and dry creek beds winding through it, so Sade often took a half hour or more to find her calves and start them back toward the lane. But she always found them, and she always bounded up to Jon when the job was done, to paw at his chest and collect her praise.

One afternoon, when Jon wasn't through with his other work by calf-fetching time, Sade went without him and brought them in alone. After that, he left the gate between the lane and the pasture open. All he had to do then was to stop the tractor when he saw Sade coming with the calves in the evening, and open the barn lot gate for them. It was an arrangement that suited him as well as Sade.

By the Fourth of July, the corn reached nearly to Jon's waist. There was little more that could be done to it, until picking time in late fall. Now was the time for a breather.

On Fourth-of-July night, the family gravitated, one by one, to the front porch. They had spent most of the day in town, watching the Jaycee parade and wandering around the Legion Park, where the carnival was set up under the trees. The Jaycees sponsored the carnival, too, and it varied little from year to year.

Jon entered the greased-pig chase as usual and failed to get anywhere near the pig as usual. For the rest of the day, he moved listlessly from one booth to another and wished he were somewhere else, doing something that would help toward getting his horse. Anything else seemed a waste of time. He was ready to go home when the rest of the family decided they'd had enough of the carnival.

"We can watch the fireworks from the front porch," Aunt Jess said on the way home. "We'll have more breeze than they'll be getting in town, and we won't have to mess with all those crowds of people."

The fireworks showed clearly beyond the Whites' barn roof, but the breeze didn't materialize. It was a heavy, hot night, with clouds rimming the horizon and sheets of heat lightning flickering beyond the front yard trees. When the fireworks were over, Aunt Jess brought out dishes of ice cream.

Jon sat on the porch railing, his back against the post, his legs balanced, one on top of the other, along the broad rail. When the ice cream came, he slid down low on his spine, so the cold dish could ride on his stomach. His skin felt clammy, although he'd taken a shower when they'd returned from town.

His back was toward the rest of them, but he could hear them. Aunt Jess was in the glider, making it creak as she moved back and forth. Dad was in the chair, with his feet against the rail behind Jon. He was quiet except for his breathing, which was loud on the exhales. Ernie was on the steps, rubbing his bare feet back and forth over the grass and humming a note or two every now and then. Elton had gone back into the house and was talking on the phone. On the porch beside Jon's leg, Sade lay panting and watching his ice cream dish.

The screen door slammed. Elton said, "I think I'll go for a drive. Cool off a little. Don't wait up."

A drive in the twins' car, with the top down, stirring up some air . . . Jon half rolled off the rail and put his dish down for Sade. "Can I come?"

Elton was already around the corner of the house. "Nope. I got a date."

"Seems kind of late to be going out," Aunt Jess said, but her voice sounded weary with the heat, too weary to object very strongly.

Ernie got up and went inside, and in a few minutes, the open bedroom window above the porch was emitting a beam of light and the static-filled sound of the ham radio. "K-Zero-R-A-V calling . . ."

Jon shut the sound out of his mind. If I had my horse, he thought, I'd go out right now and get on him, just bareback, no bridle or anything, and we'd take off down that road. Just him and me. Let those guys have their convertibles and ham shacks. Who needs 'em?

Eventually Dad and Aunt Jess went in to bed. When he ran out of things to think about, Jon went in, too, with Sade tick-tacking up the stairs behind him. He'd grown so used to having her always beside or behind or on top of him that most of the time he was unaware of her presence. But tonight he was aware, and thankful, that someone was with him.

He stripped, opened both of the windows in his room as far as they would go, and lay down on the turned-back sheets. But the room was full of collected heat, and Jon was full of feelings he couldn't pin down. After a while, he got up again, pulled on his shorts, and padded downstairs and through the kitchen to the backyard. Yawning and stretching, Sade followed.

It was cooler outside now. A breeze had finally sprung up, and it tasted damp. He swished his feet through the cool grass, tiptoed over the gravel of the lane, and stopped at the wooden gate to the cornfield.

It seemed as good a place as any to cool off. He mounted the gate and sat on top of the post, moving his feet cautiously across the rough boards to avoid splinters. Sighing, Sade dropped to the ground. She was snoring almost immediately.

After a while, he noticed that the lightning was no longer heat lightning, but the real thing, with low rumbles of thunder becoming gradually louder.

Good. We need it, he thought.

Behind him, the back door slammed. Then Ernie was leaning on the gate behind him. He was peeled down to his underwear, too.

"What ya doing out here?" Ernie's voice was low and pleasantly disinterested.

Unaware that he was whispering, Jon said, "Listening to the corn grow."

"Mmm."

They were silent then, straining their ears, trying to shut out the insects' racket and the sound of Sade's breathing. In the glow of the moonlight, the half-grown stalks of corn, row upon endless, geometric row, stirred and rippled against the breeze. The field was etched in silver and gray-green, and held the same mystery for Jon that it always did on nights like this. Between the rolls of thunder and beneath the sound of the rising wind in the trees, they could hear, faintly, the creak and rustle and murmur that was the sound of their miracle. The corn, growing.

"Ernie?"

"Mmm."

"Do you ever think about Mom much anymore?"

"Not much. Why?"

"Oh, nothing. I just wondered."

They were silent again. The wind rattled the dry leaves over their heads. The air was so thick it was almost a tangible blanket around them.

"Do you think it had anything to do with me? I mean, that she left?"

"Heck no, Jon. Where'd you ever get a stupid idea like that?"

"Oh, just—I don't know. I mean, maybe it was the idea of that *third* little kid to take care of that sort of broke the camel's back, you know? I mean . . ." He wished he hadn't said anything.

Finally Ernie said, "Quit worrying about it. It didn't have anything to do with you. She just fell in love with another guy. When you get a little older, you'll understand it."

A raindrop struck Jon on his bare kneecap. "Do you understand it, Ern?"

There was no answer. Another drop struck his chest, and then his face and shoulders. The storm was on them. Jon didn't move, and neither did Ernie. Just like the corn in front of them, Jon's skin opened to the cool, soothing rain.

After a while, he broke the silence. "I sure wish I had my horse." He sighed, long and deep, and turned his face up, squinting against the rain and opening his mouth to catch it on his tongue.

Ernie said, "I'm going in. It'll be cool enough to sleep now."

Jon climbed down and started after him, and Sade, shaking her wet coat, followed.

5

On an evening in late July, Jon wandered down to the barn, following a vague feeling that he'd just as soon be there as anywhere else. The barn was silhouetted against the soft twilight sky; the sunset was a pink reflection on its west flank. It loomed high and hip-roofed, with low wings on either side, a mother hen of a building.

Inside, it was dark. He flipped on the light, a bare yellow bulb, and began to poke into corners in a meandering way, looking for something interesting to pass the time, something he might have forgotten about.

In the back of an unused feed room off the main

area, he found it—an ancient surrey, nearly hidden behind stacks of feed bags and a welter of harness. The wheels were high; one of the shafts was broken; the body was unpainted wood, silver with age. Perched above the body was a narrow seat with peeling leather upholstery that showed stuffing and a coil of spring.

As he looked at it, Jon began to see the surrey painted and repaired and hitched to a long-legged palomino. Smiling, he stepped up into the box, arranged the reins in his hands, clucked to the horse, and sat down.

Suddenly, giant needles jabbed his bottom. He howled, threw himself down from the surrey, fell through the tangle of harness, and bolted through the barn toward the house.

A furious buzzing followed, and the needles jabbed and jabbed. From the corner of his eye, he saw Dad running after him, flailing at him with his hat. He leaped through the back door and slammed it behind him, then turned in time to see Sade leap at Dad's hand, teeth bared.

He ran out again and grabbed at the dog. "Hey, girl. Down! Did she bite you?" He was breathing heavily now, trying not to laugh or cry.

From the back porch, Aunt Jess appeared. "What in Sam Hill's going on out there!"

Jon held on to Sade, who was now jumping against his chest in a fury of excitement. His eyes met

44

Dad's. "Thanks," he breathed. "I hope she didn't bite you."

Dad rubbed his hand, where two long welts were appearing. "It's okay. You got quite a protector there. She must have thought I was beating on you, the way you were yelling."

Aunt Jess came down the steps. "Will you tell me what in the . . ."

Jon's voice was shaky, but it leaned more toward laughter now than tears. "Hornets. I sat on that old buggy in the barn. I guess they must have built a nest in the seat cushions. Man, I thought they were killing me there for a while. Dad was trying to get them off me, and I guess Sadie was trying to protect me from him."

"Hornets! Did they get your poor little seat?" She turned to go in. "Come in, and let me put some calamine lotion on. That'll take out the sting."

He glared at the back of her head as he followed her into the house. "I'll do it myself if you don't mind." His voice was cold.

"I know one thing for sure," Dad called, still rubbing his hand. "If you ever need a paddling, I'm going to tie up that dog before I start in on you."

As he passed Ernie's room on the way to the bathroom, Jon heard the twins arguing behind the closed door. They stopped talking abruptly. Then Ernie called, "What was all that yelling about down there?"

"Nothing." He reached in the medicine cabinet for the jar of calamine lotion, and hoped they'd let the subject drop. Sitting on a hornets' nest was just the sort of thing those guys would never let him live down. He breathed easier when he heard them resume their argument.

The fact that they had lowered their voices made him move more quietly as he applied the lotion to his fast-rising welts. He caught an occasional angry word, just enough to tell him they were arguing about colleges, as they had been most of the past year. He stepped into the bathtub and pressed his ear to the wall.

". . . realize, it's nearly August. We can't mess around any longer, or we're going to be out of luck at both places." It was Ernie's voice. "Just look at the difference in cost between Drake and Iowa State, the difference in tuition alone, not to mention living expenses."

"Yeah, but what's the good of going to college if you're going to live at home? That's just stupid. Besides, do you know what the ratio is at Iowa State, of girls to guys? Ten guys for every girl. Drake's got some of the classiest—"

Ernie swore sharply, then sucked in his breath and said with great control, "Look, buddy, are we going to college to learn something or to . . ." His voice sank, then rose. ". . . be stupid of me to go to

Drake just because you want to be a big man with the girls, when we've got the best agricultural college in the country just a half-hour's drive from home. The only logical thing is for you to go to Drake and me to go to Iowa State."

"No, we gotta go together. Otherwise what's the use of being twins. With both of us living down there at Drake, together, we can have a ball, switching dates, sitting in on each other's classes, and all that stuff, like we've been planning. Come on, Ern. Don't be such a horse's tail."

Standing in the bathtub with the forgotten lotion in his hand, Jon willed Ernie to fight back. He waited, but there were no sounds from Ernie's room except the occasional creak of the bedsprings.

Two months later, when the luggage-loaded convertible coasted out of the lane, it was bound for Drake University. As he waved the twins off, Jon wondered whether Ernie was still wishing he'd held out for Iowa State, or if he was really as placidly resigned as he seemed to be.

I'd never let Elton dictate to me that way, he thought savagely. Or would I? Would I be able to stand up against him any better than Ernie?

But the corn was ready for picking, and there was little time to waste thinking about the twins. Jon stayed home from school three days, and he and Dad worked furiously to get the corn in. They ate hurried, tense meals, hardly speaking to each other or to Aunt Jess.

After a few days, the strain began to show itself in Dad's temper. When Jon mentioned the horse one night at the supper table, Dad barked, "If you don't pipe down about that horse, you can just forget about it. All I've heard around here for months is that horse!"

Jon went rigid. The food in his mouth turned sour. He knew it was just the strain of getting the corn in, but he recognized the quality in Dad's voice that never appeared when he talked to the twins, a high note of barely controlled impatience, as though Dad could hardly stand to have him around and was trying not to show it. He sat perfectly still, willing the moment to pass.

As his words echoed in the quiet kitchen, Dad's neck reddened slightly. He hurried through the food that was on his plate and slammed out of the kitchen. Through the window, Jon saw him stride across the yard, stop, rub the back of his neck as he looked at the sky, and then go on more calmly toward the barn.

Winter settled in, bringing cold gray skies and a lessening of outside work to be done. Christmas was a brief bright spot that left an aftermath of sleepy depression. It seemed to Jon that time had quit moving, that there was nothing to do and nothing to look forward to.

The January mood began to work on Aunt Jess, too. One night, while she sat on the davenport watching television and knitting a sweater, she gave a snort and said, "I just made up my mind."

Jon turned from his book report on the dining room table and looked at her. Dad, behind his newspaper, said nothing.

"I just decided. I'm wasting my life away knitting sweaters that nobody ever wears. I'm going to join Cal White's square dance club."

Dad's paper collapsed. "Are you crazy? You're fif—"

"I'm two years younger than you, John, and there're lots of people in that club my age and older. Cal and Mary went for years before she passed on, and Cal's been after me for a long time to join as his partner, so he can start going again."

"But, Jess, you haven't square danced in a hundred years. Don't you think you're a little long in the tooth to be starting something as strenuous as that, for heaven's sake?"

She resumed her knitting. "I am going to do it."

Suddenly Jon grinned. "Good for you, Aunt Jess."

6

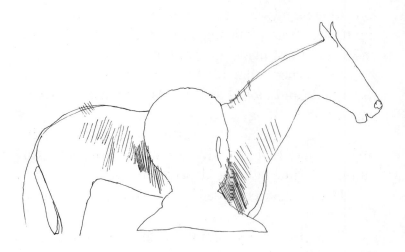

At last, Dad announced that the new pigs were ready to be marketed. On the day he took the truck-load of young hogs, including Jon's six, to the packing plant, Jon sat through his classes as though he were deaf and blind, seeing only the clock. Riding home on the bus, he stood beside the driver for a mile before the house came into sight.

He slammed the kitchen door behind him, nearly catching Sade's tail. "Hi, Dad, how much?" Panting for breath, he began to kick out of his galoshes and peel off his jacket.

Dad was at his desk in the dining room, hunched over his checkbook and the hog ledger. "Hold your horses here. I just got back a little while ago, myself. Haven't quite got this figured. Let's see. . . ."

Jon padded through the kitchen in his socks and settled in a dining room chair behind Dad. Nervously he began to pull at Sade's ears.

"Aren't you speaking to me?" Aunt Jess said from the kitchen sink, where she was peeling potatoes. The cat watched intently from the floor.

"Yeah. Hi, Aunt Jess." Jon's eyes were riveted on the scratch paper on which Dad was figuring. He half rose from his chair to crane his neck at it.

"Don't breathe down my neck, Jon. You made me lose track of my figuring, here." He retraced the problem, muttering numbers as he worked.

Jon sank back against the edge of the table and let out a long breath.

"*Minus* feed, castration, iron shots. Let's see . . . leaves you a grand total of three hundred fifty-four dollars and seventy cents." With great deliberation, Dad began to make out a check to Jon in that amount. "Now you remember what I said, buster. You don't go over a hundred and fifty on that horse, and you better plan on about a hundred or so for your school clothes next year. Here you go, mister businessman."

Jon accepted the check with mumbled thanks and floated up the stairs to his room. He sank down onto the bed. Immediately Sade was shoving in under his arm, striving for his attention. As soon as she had it, she twisted around till she was lying on her back, her head in his lap, her front legs wrapped around his arm. Automatically his hand went to her chest and began to scratch.

"We've got it now, Sadie. The hogs are sold. I've got the money right *here*. Now all we need is to find the right horse. Sadie, old girl, you're going to love it when we can go for long rides. . . ."

She had to claw at his chest to remind him to keep scratching her.

For two weeks, he watched the "Horses for Sale" ads in the paper, but there were no palominos, nothing at all that sounded interesting. He was burning to find his horse, but instead found himself at a frustrating loss about where to look.

In his concern about a horse, he almost forgot his thirteenth birthday. The birthday ritual was the same as usual, except for a surprise gift from Ernie, a pale gold bridle. The new leather smell of it nearly intoxicated him.

He hated to leave it in his room the next night. But Aunt Jess had ordered him to stay in the living room and entertain Cal White while she was upstairs putting on the final touches for her debut as a square dancer. Cal was a pleasant-looking man of fifty, nearly bald, but with the features and build of a much younger man. He didn't look quite like himself tonight, Jon thought. In his slim frontier pants with pearl-buttoned pockets, narrow fitted western shirt, and string tie, he looked as though he were dressed to play a role, and didn't care who knew it.

On his shirt was a large black plastic pin with white lettering. Jon leaned forward from his seat on the arm of the davenport, and read the pin. "Calvin White, Alamande Leftovers. Alamande *Leftovers?* That's the name of the club?" He fought down a giggle.

Cal grinned down at the pin, jutting out his jaw. "That's us. I'm sure glad Jess decided to give it a try. I've missed these Friday night dances since Mary . . ." His voice trailed off. "Had any luck yet finding a horse?"

Jon shook his head and began drumming on the end of the davenport with his heel. "Nope. I've been watching the papers, and asking around, and I tried that guy over by Boone that always has a lot of horses for sale. What's his name? Anyway, I don't know what else to do, do you?"

Cal sucked on a tooth and looked thoughtful. "Might try the sales at Ankeny. They're every other Saturday night. They get a lot of real dogs in, but once in a while you find some pretty decent animals."

"Yeah?" Jon sat up straighter.

"Tell you what." Cal thought a minute, then went on. "I might run you down there tomorrow night if you want. I *think* this is the week. Used to go down to the sales all the time, and I kind of miss them. If you don't have anything better to do, we might take a ride down and see what they got."

Jon's face lit up. He started to answer, but Aunt Jess was coming through the door, and Cal turned away.

She wore a turquoise squaw dress trimmed with silver rickrack. On her feet were flat black shoes Jon had never seen. He had expected her to look at least slightly ridiculous. He had his smart remarks prepared, but somehow the outfit didn't look out of place at all. Her frame was big-boned but not heavy, and with her dark McBride coloring and chiseled features, the squaw dress was oddly compatible.

"You look real nice, Aunt Jess." The words were as surprising to Jon as they were to Aunt Jess, but she looked so pleased he was glad he hadn't teased her. He followed them to the back door.

"You kids have a good time, now, and no parking to neck on the way home."

Cal turned to grin over his shoulder at Jon. "Smart-aleck kid. Pick you up about six tomorrow night?"

It had been dark for almost two hours when Cal White's truck pulled into the parking lot outside the Ankeny Livestock Pavilion. The broad lot was already nearly filled with stock trucks, slat-boarded pickups, cars, horse trailers, even a few motorcycles. The building loomed above the vehicles, huge and indistinct in the dark. In the near corner of the building were large brightly lighted windows that showed Jon the booths and counters of a small cafe.

He followed Cal through the cafe door. It was a large concrete-floored room, paneled in knotty pine and filled with noise and smoke and Levi-clad people. From somewhere beyond, he heard the chant of the auctioneer. His heart sank.

"Sounds like they've already started," he said to the back of Cal's jacket. Maybe his dream horse was here, and was sold already. He felt a gnawing irritation at Cal for not getting here earlier.

Cal held open a door at the back of the cafe. "Nah. They always do the tack and junk first. It'll be a good hour before they get around to the horses."

They went through a cold-floored hallway, past cigarette and popcorn machines and rest rooms. Then Cal veered left through broad swinging doors, and they were in the arena. They went uphill, between the bleachers that rose on either side, then stopped for a moment at the crest of the concrete slope.

Below them was the ring, a small tanbark circle with a raised stage at the back. People were milling around in the ring, examining used saddles, pieces of harness, aluminum water buckets, currycombs, even a few pair of boots. The auctioneer, a ruddy-faced young man in a red plaid jacket, was holding up a pair of reins.

"Lookie here, a dandy pair of braided rawhide reins. You need 'em for that western pleasure outfit.

Brand new, never been used. Who'll start me out with a dollar?"

"Let's go take a look at the horses," Jon said. Cal began to move again, down the ramp, around the narrow aisle between the bottom row of bleachers and the ring's rail. They pushed through a door in the back wall of the arena, and Jon found himself in the barn. His heart began to pound. Maybe somewhere in here . . .

Cal stopped to talk to someone, so Jon edged around him and started down the aisle, turning his head quickly from side to side, looking for a palomino. A small pinto with rolling eyes came skittering down the aisle toward him, bearing a huge man whose elbows flapped like turkey wings. Jon stepped aside.

The barn was even colder than the arena had been. At the far end of the aisle, the doors stood open, showing the black night sky and a maze of stock pens. Inside, the barn was dirt-floored and lighted, none too well, by high bare yellow light bulbs. The aisles ran in an H, with box stalls along the outer walls and larger pens in between the two long aisles. There seemed to be at least one or two horses in every stall.

He made a fast trip through first, then went back to the one horse that looked promising. Since the animal was tied at the back of the stall, in the shadows, Jon opened the stall gate and went inside. The horse lifted his head and stared down at the boy.

"Hey, you're a big one, aren't you?" Jon's voice

was soft as his eyes traveled over the animal.

He was a copper-bright palomino, long-legged and somehow sleek-looking, even in his winter coat. His neck was long and well shaped, his head large but not coarse. Although his tail was carried high, the white strands fell nearly to the floor. His mane was long; his forelock came almost to his nostrils.

Recognition broke over Jon as he stared at the horse. This is the one.

He ran his hand down the long neck, over the shoulders. The horse showed no reaction.

"Find a prospect, did you?" Cal came into the stall behind Jon. "Lord, he's a big guy. I bet he'll stand seventeen hands. Why don't you try him out, if you like the looks of him?"

If I like the looks of him! Jon thought. What do you mean "if"?

"I'll go see if I can find out who owns him," Cal said. He left, and came back a few minutes later with the large man Jon had seen earlier on the pinto.

"That's quite a hunk of horse, ain't he?" the man said. "He's half saddle-bred, half Wyoming ranch horse, with a little Arab blood in there somewhere. Comin' six-year-old, and as good-broke a horse as you'll ever find. Try him out if you want."

Jon nodded. Suddenly he wished he'd taken time to go to the rest room first.

The man untied the lead rope, tossed it over the horse's neck, and tied the loose end through the halter ring. "Gimme your foot." He grabbed Jon's ankle and hoisted him up.

"Take him out back," the man said. "He'll neck rein."

Jon looked down at the two men. He felt very high and not at all secure. But here was his horse under him. He took the rope in one hand and a fistful of mane in the other, and reined the horse through the stall gate into the aisle. The body beneath him rocked along at a tense but smooth walk. The head in front of him was high, alert, ready to be frightened. Testing, Jon pulled lightly on the halter rope, and the horse stopped immediately. At a touch of Jon's heels, they were moving again.

At the barn door, Jon ducked low. Then they were outside. He relaxed and began to feel as though he were in command. There was a long alleyway that led away from the barn, between rows of white-boarded stock pens. High lights and the cold stars threw shadows across the alley. A few people walked or rode or stood. Jon felt as though they were all looking at his horse, maybe thinking of bidding for him.

With aching lungs filled with cold air, he clamped his legs tight around the horse's barrel. They lunged forward in a loping canter. Up and down the alley they went, weaving around other riders, cantering, walking, trotting, both horse and rider breathing clouds of frost against the black sky. Although the horse seemed reluctant to slow down, he obeyed the

58

flimsy pressure of the halter each time Jon pulled. Finally, when the muscles in Jon's thighs ached with weakness, he headed back into the barn.

Cal was watching from the door. "Looked to me like he handled pretty good for you, Jonnie. How does he feel to you?"

"Feels okay." He dropped to the ground, stumbling backward, and handed the lead rope back to the horse's owner. "What's his name?"

"Prince." The man turned and led the big gelding back into the stall.

Prince. Jon shuddered. I'll have to change that.

Suddenly he remembered the hundred and fifty dollar limit Dad had set. He felt sick. If the bidding went over that . . .

"We better go get a seat," Cal said. "They've already started on the horses."

The steep bleachers that encircled the arena were packed full by now. Jon left Cal in the crowd that stood four deep around the rail, and made his way to the men's room. There was a line. He fretted at the slowness of it, sure that his horse would be sold while he stood out here in the blasted line.

But after he'd rejoined Cal at the ring, he faced a nerve-stretching wait of more than an hour before the arena door admitted the palomino. The horse swung easily around the tight circle, head high, dark eyes surveying the crowd.

He's looking for me, Jon thought. No, that's

silly. But—if I don't get that horse . . . Already the
bitterness of the disappointment was rising from his
stomach.

"How high can you go?" Cal murmured.

"Hundred and fifty. What do you think?"

Cal looked thoughtful and sucked his tooth.

The auctioneer cleared his throat loudly over the
mike. "All right now, here we have what y'all have
been lookin' for. Here's a western pleasure horse,
parade horse, something nice for the wife and kids, as
sound and good-broke as anything you'll ever ride.
Comin' six-year-old this spring, gentle as an old lady.
Ain't he about the prettiest thing you ever saw?"

Lay off the sales pitch, will you, Jon prayed. His
eyes left the horse long enough to scan the faces behind and above him. He couldn't read them through
the smoke that hung in the air.

In the ring, the horse's owner had vaulted astride
and was driving the animal forward, holding him back,
turning him, backing him with heavy use of the halter
and lead rope. The gelding responded with arched
neck and high tail and beautifully nervous side steps.

Don't look so good. Jon's hands clamped rigidly
around the metal rail.

"Now, folks, you're not going to want to pass
this one up. Who'll start me with a hundred now?
Who'll . . ."

Cal's hand came down hard on Jon's arm as it
started up to bid.

"We ain't going to *give* this horse away, folks. Now who'll start me with eighty, eighty, eighty . . ."

A hand somewhere to the left of Jon shot up. On the floor of the ring, a young man who seemed to be assisting the auctioneer spotted the hand and pointed at it dramatically, holding his point like a bird dog until the auctioneer noted the bid.

"We got eighty, eighty now. Who'll gimme five, eighty-five . . ."

Jon's arm shot up. The assistant pointed.

"Eighty-five now. Who'll make it ninety . . ."

Another hand, another dramatic point.

"Ninety now. Who'll make it one, one, one? Now who'll make it one . . ."

Jon waved again. His heart was pounding a sickening beat that sent waves all through his body.

"One now. One ten, who'll gimme one ten, one ten?" The chant began to hypnotize Jon.

The assistant, grinning now, jabbed his pointing finger away from Jon, then spun back to stare into Jon's eyes. The whole thing began to take on a dreamlike quality.

"Twenty now. Who'll make it thirty . . ." Jon's arm rose. "Thirty—thirty—thirty—thirty once . . ." Suddenly Jon felt a crazy desire to run out, to find the rest room again, to escape the crushing disappointment that was flying at his face.

The pointer spun when a voice bellowed, "One forty."

Pointer and auctioneer looked back at Jon. "Forty-five?" Jon nodded, raising his hand needlessly. Here it comes. Here it comes. . . .

"You gonna let this youngster steal your horse for a measly one forty-five?" The auctioneer spoke in the direction of the other bidder. "Make it fifty, now fifty, now fifty . . ."

The pointer picked up the man's bid. Nausea began to roll over Jon as the attention of the men in the ring swung back to him.

"You gonna let this big bully steal your horse for a measly one fifty, kid? Gimme fifty-five, now five, now five . . ."

Suddenly Jon's arm was dangling above his head, held up by Cal's grip.

"Fifty-five now. Who'll make it sixty?" The silence was deafening. The pointer pivoted, watched, but did not point. "I got one fifty-five. Once . . . twice . . . last chance now . . . They used to hang men for horse stealing, and you're letting this boy steal that horse at this price. . . . Sold."

For just an instant, the room swung before Jon's gaze. Then Cal's hand was in the small of his back, steering him toward the exit and the cashier's window. He felt Cal slip a bill into his hand. Through the ringing in his ears, he heard Cal mutter, "I sure hope we got enough gas in the truck to get home on."

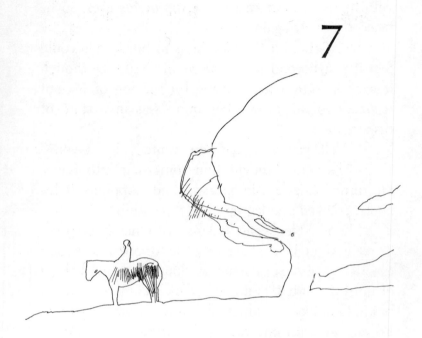

7

It began to spit snow on the drive home, small hard flakes that were swept off the highway by gusts of wind as soon as they hit. They made a diagonal white-on-black pattern in the truck's headlights. It was so warm inside the cab that Jon shed his gloves and jacket. The radio was playing "I Didn't Know Angels Ever Walked on This Earth" from a high-power station in Del Rio, Texas.

Jon turned again to stare through the window behind his head. Between the boards of the truck's body, he could make out segments of the horse's front legs just above the knees. He felt Cal watching him with amusement from the corners of his eyes, so he faced the front again.

He waited for the happiness to break. He could feel it just beyond the reach of his mind, as though it were holding back, waiting for the fog of his not *realizing* to roll away. His mind was in a state of suspension.

"Well, you got what you wanted, didn't you?"

Cal's voice brought him somewhat into focus. He turned sideways in the seat and, slipping off his boots, crooked one leg up onto the cushion.

"Yep." He began talking with nervous speed. "I really thought I'd have to settle for one that wasn't exactly . . . I mean I've always known just what kind of horse I wanted, you know, dark palomino, real big but not chunky, a gelding. But I didn't honestly think I'd end up with one that had everything I wanted."

Cal smiled. They rode in silence.

"I'll pay you back the five dollars. Cal— thanks . . ."

"Ahh." Cal's hand waved away Jon's thanks.

It was nearly one o'clock when they turned in at the McBride mailbox. The only light came from the kitchen windows, but as the truck turned by the barn and backed up to the loading chute, the yard light and the yellow bulb over the barn door blinked on, and Dad and Aunt Jess started across the yard. They wore heavy jackets over robes over pajamas, and Aunt Jess had on a pair of the twins' galoshes.

As Jon jumped down from the truck, Sade threw herself at his chest, whining with joy. He ruffed her coat automatically, then dropped her and ran to the tailgate.

"I got one." He beamed back over his shoulder at Dad and Aunt Jess. "Just wait till you see this. Grab Sadie, Aunt Jess. I don't want her scaring him."

His fingers were stiff with cold and excitement. He couldn't get the tailgate pin undone on his side. Cal came around and worked it free for him. Then the gate was off, and he was untying his horse's lead rope. He led him down the chute and into the yellow circle of light by the barn.

A tingling awakening sensation was coming over him now. Everything in the line of his vision came into intense focus—the horse's huge gold head above his shoulder, with its bony planes and meandering blood vein, and the white grains of snow that sat so lightly on the tips of the furry winter hair; the dark cracked leather of the halter; the boards of the barn and the movement of the snow through the light. He forgot to breathe. The happiness came and lodged in his throat.

Aunt Jess said, "He's a beauty, Jonnie. What's his name?"

Dad moved close and, turning his back to Jon, ran an expert hand over the horse's near front leg. The hand tugged at the wisp of fetlock hair, and obligingly the horse shifted his weight and allowed

Dad to pick up his hoof. Slowly Dad made his way around the animal, eyeing pasterns, the set of the head, the slope of the shoulders, ears and eyes, and front-end squareness. He ended his inspection by separating the horse's lips with a flick of his thumb.

Finally he spoke. "How much you give for him?"

"Hundred and fifty . . . five. I didn't think you'd mind if it was just five dollars over." He held his breath.

"Mm-hm. Well, looks like you did all right. Course you can't tell, buying through an auction like that. He may have faults that won't show up till later. From the looks of things, though, I'd say he's probably worth the money. Cal, you want a cup of coffee before you go?"

As the three of them turned to go in, Sade broke free from Aunt Jess and bounded at Jon. She barked. The horse flung back his head, dragging Jon back a step. Nostrils flared, and huge dark eyes rolled toward the dog, showing white rims.

"No, no, Sade! Get away!" Jon's voice struck the dog visibly. "Aunt Jess, take her with you! She's scaring the horse! Get away!" He turned his attention to the horse, who had already quieted down. He didn't notice the puzzled tilt of Sade's head, or the way her tail slowly ceased to wag.

"Come along, Sadie girl. Come with me, and we'll get you a milk bone." Aunt Jess snapped her fingers, and Sade turned and followed her reluctantly into the house.

Inside the barn, Jon tied the horse in a stall that had been made ready two weeks ago. "I'm sorry we don't have box stalls, fella. But I'll come down first thing in the morning and let you run in the barn lot."

He reached up to wrap his arm around the horse's neck and realized for the first time that the ridge of backbone was well above the top of his head. For an instant, he buried his nose in the furry shoulder. It smelled of warmth and dust.

"Good night, My Horse," whispered Jon.

The gelding lowered his head to the hay and began to eat.

Sun God. The name came to Jon literally in a dream, and was waiting in his consciousness when he woke.

"Yes—Sun God. Sunny. He whispered it in the empty bedroom. "The perfect name for the perfect horse."

From his bed, he could look out the window and see the hip-roofed bulk of the barn in the gray winter morning. There had been only enough snow last night to fill the frozen ruts of the lane and to gather in clumps of dead grass between the buildings. As he sat up to look out the window, Sade raised her head and watched him expectantly.

"Okay, Sadie, let's get up." The warm weight of her left his leg. She hit the floor, then watched, bright-eyed, over the edge of the bed while he did his last stretching and savoring of the warmth of the covers. He dressed standing over the register and made his way quietly down the stairs and through the kitchen. The kitchen clock said seven-ten.

At the barn door, he stopped and held Sade back with a hand against her chest. "You better stay away from Sun God till he gets a little more used to things, Sadie. Go on back to the house. I'll be back in an hour or so." He opened the door a crack and slipped in, shutting it before she could follow.

Sun God was watching him. "Morning, fella. Did you have a good night?" He led the horse through the door at the end of the aisle and turned him loose in the small high-fenced lot. Sun God trotted away, head low, mane shaking.

"Go ahead and stretch the old legs, Sunny. I'll clean out your stall, and then we'll go for a ride." When he turned to go back into the barn, he saw Sade watching through the lot fence.

He cleaned out the stall, dumped a fresh arm-load of hay in the manger, then lifted his tack from the saddle rack he'd built on the wall. The pale gold leather of his new bridle contrasted with the battered, age-blackened army saddle that he'd unearthed last summer in a dark corner of the feed room.

This is it, he thought, staring in wonder at the

tack. I'm going out to saddle my horse for a little early-morning gallop before breakfast. It's coming true.

He set the equipment on the ground beside the barn and turned to the horse, one hand extended.

"Okay, boy. Come on. Let's go."

His hand was almost on the halter when Sun God swerved and trotted away. For several minutes, they played a game of touch-me-not, while Jon's face became set, his voice grim. At length, the horse turned away to stand with his head in the corner of the fence. When Jon tried to move up beside him, the high gold hindquarters moved deftly to block him. He felt sickened.

Finally, on an inspiration, he got an ear of corn from the barn and stood in the center of the lot, holding it out. Sun God spotted it, watched it for a minute, then slowly came out of his corner to get it. Jon held onto the corn until his other hand had a secure grip on Sun God's halter.

"There now, you so and so, I got you, didn't I?" The sick sensation faded, and the sun touched the barn lot with its first long rays.

There was no problem with the saddle. It was a McClellan, with a two-inch-wide split down the center, a high pommel and cantle, and heavy wooden stirrups that hung on narrow leathers. The split settled securely over the ridge of Sun God's spine, and the girth proved uncomplicated, even though Jon had never actually saddled a horse before.

The bridle was more difficult. He held it as the books said to, warming the bit in his hands, but when the metal touched Sun God's lips, the horse's head moved up, high out of reach. Finally Jon had to climb up onto the fence to which the halter rope was tied. With the advantage of this added height, the battle was soon won.

He was mounted and starting Sun God down the lane toward the pasture when he heard Sade's yip behind him. He turned just as she clawed under the fence and bounded across the lot.

"No, no, Sade! Go home! Go on! You can't come."

Suddenly the horse leaped forward. Jon grabbed the flying mane and managed to hang on until he had his balance. Sun God answered the pull on the reins by settling into a jog. Gradually Jon's heart slowed to normal, and he began breathing again. When he ventured a look back over his shoulder, Sade was standing at the foot of the lane.

They rode all the way around the pasture, down gullies, across dry creek beds, around clumps of sumac and elm shoots, up steep wooded slopes. In the open places, Jon let Sun God canter for short stretches, always pulling him up when he felt himself losing his balance. Each time the horse obeyed his command, Jon felt a glow, a sort of expansion.

Once Sun God made a sudden sideways movement when a rabbit exploded from the brush beside him. Jon was thrown up onto his neck, but managed to hang on.

He began to sing, likening himself to the happy cowboy described in the lyrics. Sun God was moving at a prancing gait that was half walk, half trot, and it exactly matched the beat of the song.

His thoughts followed the rhythm. Oh, man. This is what I wanted, and I got it. I'll never be as happy again in my whole life as I am right now. The knowledge saddened him.

The cold was beginning to make itself felt. His fingers were stiff, and a bead of moisture hung from the tip of his nose. He turned his horse toward home. At the top of his lungs, he sang about the glories of the Old West, where a man and his horse could roam free.

8

In the weeks that followed, Jon's schedule adjusted itself to Sun God. He got up half an hour earlier each morning to get in a quick ride before chicken chores and school. After school, he brushed Sun God, combed the tangles out of the long mane and tail, filled the manger, the grain box, and the water bucket, and then, if it was still light enough outside, went for another short ride before supper.

Sade was allowed inside the barn while Jon did the feeding and grooming. She lay against the wall across the aisle from Sun God's stall, close yet out of the way. But she was not allowed to follow when Jon and the horse started out the pasture lane.

Sade was restricted because she made Sunny nervous, Jon told himself, and because the horse might take a kick at her and hurt her. He couldn't quite bring himself to admit that his fear might be for himself.

He'd fallen off three times now—twice when Sade had started to follow Sunny and the horse literally jumped out from under his rider; once when Sun God had spooked at some movement in the cornfield. He'd galloped full out, down the lane and into the barn lot, swerving at the gate and losing Jon. The spills had knocked the wind out of Jon and bruised him a little on an elbow or a shoulder, nothing to worry about.

But with each fall, he became more aware of a feeling of fear, not fear of the horse or of being hurt, but a fear that someday he *might* be afraid to get back on.

Every horseman takes some spills, he assured himself. You have to if you want to learn to ride. And it certainly isn't Sunny's fault if I can't stay on him.

In April, the twins came home for spring vacation. As soon as they had changed into old clothes, they followed Jon down to the lot to see the horse. They watched over the fence for a few minutes. Then Ernie said, "Let's try him out."

Jon ducked through the fence and, holding his

breath, approached Sun God. "Come on, fella. Show 'em how nice you can be, *please.*" He spoke silently.

Sun God didn't want to be caught. Jon's heart sank as the horse turned away from his hand and trotted through the gate and up the lane.

"He doesn't want to go to work very bad, does he?" Elton called, laughing.

Jon clenched his teeth and started up the lane after Sunny. When the halter was finally in his grasp, he led the horse back to the barn more brusquely than usual.

Jon felt almost a physical pain when Elton swung up into the saddle and cantered away. He watched while both of the twins rode, with far more assurance than he ever did. Then he followed them silently back to the house.

That night, coming out of the bathroom, he heard Elton and Ernie talking in Elton's room. The word *horse* halted him outside the bedroom door. He cocked his head and listened.

". . . good-looking horse, but I think baby brother bit off a little more than he can chew." It was Elton.

"Oh, I don't know. Sunny behaved all right when I was riding him. Tried the old bolting-back-toward-the-barn trick, but I didn't have any real trouble holding him."

"Yeah, Ern, but you and I are a darn sight stronger than Jon, and we've been riding for years. The kid's just a beginner. He should have gotten a real nice, quiet old horse with a lot of years behind it."

"Ahh, you're just looking for trouble. That's not a mean horse."

Elton's voice rose. "I never said he was *mean.* I just don't think he's a kid's horse, that's all."

Burning with hurt and anger, Jon moved down the hall to his room. He swore silently. The high and mighty nerve of those guys! What do they know about Sunny, anyhow? They ride him for about ten minutes, and they're experts. Those stupid, stupid . . . He flung himself across the bed and absentmindedly pulled Sade against his chest.

Elton's words soured Jon's sleep that night, and hung with him when he went out to the barn lot the next morning to get Sunny. Sade followed him as far as the fence and watched through the boards while he fought his way across the muddy lot toward the horse. He felt an unreasoning irritation when Sun God evaded his grasp.

"All right, all right. Corn." He slogged back to the barn for the ear of corn that had become Sun God's prerequisite to being caught.

He tied Sunny in the narrow stall and got the currycomb and brush. The barn was warm enough this morning that he could work comfortably without gloves. His hands felt free and light, and his mood began to lift. He could hear Sade scratching at the front door of the barn, but his arms were moving in such even, rhythmic strokes down Sunny's neck that he didn't want to stop to open the door.

He coughed. The cloud of dust that rose from his brush was thick with yellow hair. After a few minutes, he paused, waved away the dust, and peered at Sunny's neck. Through the thinning winter coat shone a gloss of darker gold, fine short slick hair. He sighed, then unzipped his jacket and went to work on the muscled ridges of Sunny's shoulder. Sade was at the back door now, the one that led to the lot. She whined, clawed at the door, jumped up against it.

"Wonder what's eating her this morning, Sunny? I'll have to go let her in in a minute." But the winter hair was coming off even better over the horse's ribs. He was mesmerized by the transformation.

Suddenly the barn door creaked open, and Sade padded in, her legs and chest dripping mud from the lot. She stood behind Sunny, wagging uncertainly at Jon, then sank into her spot beside the opposite wall. The barn door creaked on its hinges.

For a moment, Jon's brushes slowed. "How'd you do that, Sadie?" She raised her head and wagged her tail. "Did you open that door? You must have." It was a crossbar latch on the outside, he mused. She was probably just jumping up and clawing at the door and accidentally pulled down on the end of the crossbar. Easy enough. Briefly he felt good that Sade had wanted in where he was badly enough to have done that. Then he turned his attention back to the job at hand.

He was digging the brush into Sunny's hips when, abruptly, the hips moved toward him. "Feels pretty good, huh, boy?" But before the words were out, he felt himself being tipped back against the stall partition. The point of Sun God's hip was against his nose and mouth. A hot wash of panic poured over him. Instinctively he brought his left hand up hard, driving the bristles of the brush into Sun God's belly. The hips swung away.

Jon looked at Sunny's head. The ears were half cocked back; the head was turned slightly. One brown eye watched him.

Unreasonably, he wanted to cry.

Instead, he finished brushing Sunny's left side and went around to do the other. As he came out of the stall, his eyes met Ernie's. He flushed.

"Does he always crowd like that in the stall?" Ernie said quietly.

Jon went to Sunny's mane, lifted it, and began to brush. "He wasn't crowding. That was just this little game he plays. Just messing around. He and I . . ." He broke off and concentrated on his brushing, working faster now and praying it wouldn't happen again with Ernie standing there. He was furious with Ernie for hanging around anyway, but thankful it had been Ernie instead of Elton.

He put the bridle on Sun God and led him out

to the front of the barn. "Give me a leg up, Ernie," he called.

"Aren't you going to use the saddle?" Ernie tossed him up.

"Nah. Just gets in the way." So I'm showing off, he thought. So what?

As he sat there, looking down into Ernie's face beside his knee, he felt suddenly tall. Sun God's power was his as long as he was astride. He could boot Sunny into a gallop and leave Ernie just standing there.

Abruptly he reined Sunny around and clapped his heels in hard. Across the turnaround they clattered, then around the chicken house, along the edge of the orchard, and through the open gate of the hayfield.

His jacket flapped back around his arms. He sat tall and straight with his rein hand low in front of him, the other arm hanging close to his side. The hayfield was a low stubble over soft gray clods of earth. Soft landing just in case. The ground rolled gently, giving Sunny's rocking-chair canter the swoop of a merry-go-round. His face was full of sunlight and wet spring air.

Sunny shied lightly at a pheasant, and Jon's body followed the smooth side step as though they were dancing. Suddenly he stuck his tongue out—at Elton and Ernie and the whole world.

A few days later, while the twins were still on vacation, Dad took the two of them to Missouri to buy calves. It was earlier than he liked to buy them; he would have to feed them hay for a few weeks until the pasture was ready. But he wanted to get it done while the boys could go, and before plowing started, for only Dad and Jon would be doing the field work this year.

They were gone three days. When the two stock trucks pulled in on Thursday evening, Jon and Sade were waiting beside the lot fence.

As the first calf clattered down the chute, Sade slipped through the fence and became a cattle dog again. But Jon's eyes were on Sun God. The horse was going to have to share his quarters with about forty adolescent cows, and Jon had some misgivings about Sunny's graciousness.

But Sun God stood aloof, ignoring the calves even when they came close. Jon relaxed and went into the house.

After supper, he and Ernie set up the chessboard in the middle of the living room floor and settled on either side of it with a bowl of popcorn, paper napkins, and bottles of Pepsi that had half-frozen in the refrigerator, just the way Jon loved them.

He was a little surprised at how glad he was to have Ernie there, playing their old blood-and-guts chess. Every few years one of them got on a chess kick. Then, for weeks at a time, the chessboard sat ready on the dining room buffet for their after-supper game. Of course, the chess games had become less frequent after Ernie got his ham radio three years ago. And then, with the twins away at college, they had ceased altogether.

Elton had a date that night, and Dad went to bed right after supper, worn out from his long drive. Aunt Jess settled on the davenport to divide her attention between the chess game and the television.

"What ails that dog, Jon?" she said, as Sade paced from the cedar chest window seat to the front door, to Jon, and back to the window.

Jon was studying the board. "I don't know. I guess she's just antsy about the calves. Your move." He scooped up a handful of popcorn and tossed a kernel to Sade, never taking his eyes away from Ernie's hand, hovering over a rook.

Finally Sade flopped down beside Jon and worked her head under his arm and into his lap. His fingers began massaging the ruff of her neck. She sighed and braced one paw against his shirt front and closed her eyes.

Ernie moved his rook. Jon held his breath, moved a pawn. Ernie pondered for a long moment, then slowly, cautiously moved a bishop.

"Yahoo!" Jon whooped. "Check and checkmate. Man, did you ever leave yourself wide open for that one. Hoo-eee!" He rolled over on his back, and immediately Sade was on top of him, tail thrashing, paws digging at his chest as her tongue sought his face. "Sadie, you old hound, you're gorgeous."

It was their first good wrestle in weeks.

Since Sun God.

9

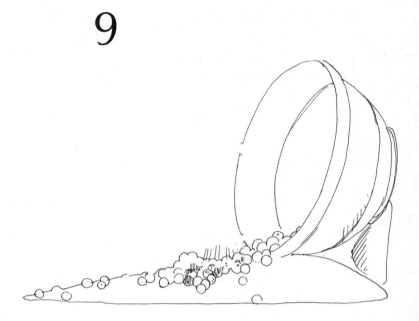

The next morning Sade was up at daylight, digging at the covers to wake Jon. He tried for a while to ignore her but finally gave in and groped his way downstairs, his eyes still squinted shut. He opened the back door to let her out, then stumbled back upstairs. There was still a half hour before he had to get up.

But by the time he'd burrowed back under the covers, his mind was finished with sleeping. He sat up and pulled the blankets around his neck. Outside, he could see Sade trotting toward her calves. He smiled.

You're too early, Sade, he thought. I'll be darned if I'm coming down there and open the gate, just so you can play cowboy.

As he watched, the white form of Sade moved in among the calves and paused beside the gate that led into the pasture lane. She stood irresolutely looking from the gate to the house for several minutes. At length, she began to jump against the gate, nosing toward the loop of wire that held it shut. Jon couldn't see the wire from where he watched, and Sade was only a pale dog-shaped blob, but after she'd made a few fruitless lunges at the gate, he saw it swing open. Very faintly its creaking came through the morning stillness.

Jon buried his chin in the blankets over his knees. He watched with interest while Sade wheeled around the calves and started them down the lane. Only then did it occur to him that Sade was letting Sun God out, too.

He considered for a minute, then shrugged back down into the bed. I couldn't get down there in time to stop him, anyway. Just hope I don't have too much trouble catching him after school. He was just dozing off when Aunt Jess called him to get up.

That afternoon, when he and Sade went to bring in the calves, Jon took his bridle and three ears of corn. It took him more than a half hour to find Sun God and coax him within grabbing range with the corn. Several minutes later he had won the bridling struggle; Sun God took advantage of the fact that his head wasn't tied down, and persisted in holding it high above Jon's reach. Then it took a while to find a log to use for a mounting block. By the time he was finally mounted, Sade had already gathered the calves and started them down the lane toward the barn.

The air was chilling by now. Sun God flexed his neck and snatched nervously at the bit. Jon held him to a walk, but the walk became a two-step as the barn came in sight at the end of the lane.

The herd that clogged the lane ahead reminded Jon of the late movie he and Ernie had stayed up to watch last night. Robert Mitchum, driving the long-horns across Kansas or somewhere.

Suddenly Sun God lunged forward. He galloped flat out, head low, exploding through the calves and nearly trampling Sade.

"Hey. Whoa. Easy there."

But the barn was ahead, and the bit was in Sunny's teeth. Jon braced with one arm against a fistful of mane while he hauled back on the reins. With each leap, his balance slipped a little more.

At the lot gate, Sunny swerved so sharply that only the grit of Jon's teeth kept him on the horse's back. The form of one of the twins flashed across Jon's vision. Then the barn was dead ahead.

The door stood open. The black shape of it flew toward him. He couldn't scream; the wind was too strong against his face. He threw himself forward along Sunny's neck, and at that instant they clattered through the blackness of the barn.

Immediately Sun God churned to a halt. At his stall, he turned in. Before the echo of his hooves on the floor had died, the long head was lowered into the manger.

As Jon slid trembling to the floor, Elton came through the door. "You all right?" he demanded.

Jon nodded and turned his back to Elton. His fingers shook as he fought with the buckle on the bridle's throatlatch.

"You could have had your darn-fool head knocked off, I hope you realize."

Jon turned. Despite the difference in their heights, he looked levelly into his brother's eyes. "No, I wouldn't have. That was just a sort of game Sunny and I play. He wouldn't hurt me. This horse loves me, Elton. So just mind your own business."

The June sun burned on the back of his neck and the rims of his ears as Jon squatted beside the raspberry bushes. He could feel his skin growing tender around the cowlick at the back of his head, and he knew he was in for a sunburned scalp. A mosquito jabbed his neck. He hunched his shoulder fiercely in the direction of the sting. Then his fingers pried gently, and another raspberry pulled loose from its stem and fell into the plastic dishpan in the crook of his arm. He felt as though he'd been picking all morning, and yet the bottom of the dishpan was just now disappearing from sight.

He sighed. In the grass lay the bridle and an ear of corn. Somewhere in the pasture, maybe quite close, Sun God was waiting for him. His irritation at the berry-picking was augmented by the sound of the Deere's motor growing louder, then fainter, in the cornfield.

Resentfully he thought, Old Elton's out there on *my* tractor, doing *my* cultivating, while *I* get stuck with a stupid job like picking raspberries. Honest to Pete!

Sade raised her head from the grass, looked at him, then lay back down. Her tail thumped once.

As he moved to the next clump of bushes, his foot came within inches of a mammoth bull snake dozing in the sun. He and the snake exchanged long stares.

"Well. Ferdinand the bull snake," he said. "The farmer's little friend. Why don't you go catch mice or rats or whatever, like you're supposed to, and stay out of my way?"

The snake drew itself up slightly. Suddenly the ugliness of the snake disgusted him. He wanted to hurt it, to hurt something.

"Sade! Come here and get the snake! Go on. Get it." But by the time Sade had yawned, stretched, risen, and trotted over, the bull snake had disappeared beneath the raspberry bushes.

"Boy, great white hunter. Fat lot of help you are." She wagged and looked up at him, and automatically his hand found the itchy place on her neck.

Sighing again, he went back to work. A while later he heard the pickup creaking and jouncing across the rough ground of the pasture somewhere behind him. He turned to look, but a spur of trees and brush separated him from the sound. Not far away the truck stopped. The door slammed. Someone whistled.

Must be Ernie bringing salt for the calves, he decided.

Sade rose and trotted around the edge of the timber toward the sound. It occurred to Jon that if he got enough berries picked before the truck left, Ernie could take the pan back to the house for him. Then he wouldn't have to bother trying to bring it in on horseback and maybe spill the berries. He began to pick as swiftly as he could.

As he worked, he listened for the sound of the pickup starting, so he could run around the trees and yell to Ernie, if necessary. Instead of the truck, he suddenly heard loud, angry barking.

Sadie? he wondered. He set down the dishpan and loped through the long grass, around the trees and underbrush. He rounded the corner just as Sade snarled and edged toward Sun God's head. She didn't jump, but moved in a menacing half-crouch, ears flattened, still barking furiously.

The horse and half a dozen calves stood near the huge pink block of salt that Ernie had just rolled from the truck. Sun God's neck was arched unnaturally high. His ears were flattened. His eyes showed white, and he seemed to be standing on tiptoe. The calves had backed off to watch.

As soon as the scene impressed itself on Jon's mind, he rushed in. "Damn you, Sade! Stop it! What's the matter with you?" His hand came down twice with all his strength on her rump.

Instantly she turned from the horse to Jon, whining softly.

"Don't hit her," Ernie shouted. "You stupe. She was just protecting her calves. Why don't you find out what's going on before you jump in and start beating dogs?"

Jon looked up at him. His hand burned where he'd pounded Sade. "What do you mean?"

Ernie came around the pickup and explained with exaggerated patience. "I was bringing out this new salt block for the calves, and that littlest calf over there—well, in fact all the calves—were trying to get up to it. Only your horse came along like king of the road and shoved the calves away from the block. That little calf tried to get in his licks anyway, and Sun God squealed and took a bite out of his neck, and that's when good old Sadie there took out after him. And then *you* come barging in and start beating on the poor dog, just because she was trying to do her job taking care of the calves."

"Oh." Jon stood uneasily while Ernie drove off. Then he leaned over and stroked Sade's head quickly, without meeting her eyes.

On his way back to the raspberries, he stopped for a minute to watch his horse grazing. Sun God was incredibly golden against the deep bright green of the grass and the brilliant June sky. His coat gleamed so that it was almost painful to look at. The long cream mane and tail rippled in the breeze. He lifted his head from the grass and looked at Jon from behind the luxurious fall of his forelock.

An ache began to grow in Jon's chest. It lodged in his throat.

10

Supper had been over for an hour or more, but it was still bright daylight. For the first time since the twins had come home a week ago, the entire family sat together in front of the house, not saying much, watching the sun get lower and redder. Aunt Jess swung lazily in the swing. The twins sprawled down the steps of the porch. Dad sat in the old awning-striped lawn chair.

Jon sat in the grass between Dad and the twins, aware that he was probably getting chiggers, but not much caring. He looked down at the long purple raspberry stains on his T-shirt, and the purple rims of his fingernails, and shrugged them off. Near his feet, Sade lay on her back, head twisted to one side, front paws tucked up coyly, hind legs flopping. As his bare toes found her wishbone and began to rub, she moved her tail through the grass. One hind leg jerked as he touched an itchy spot.

The twins were murmuring behind Jon, so low he caught only an occasional word. He felt an unreasonable irritation toward them, toward the mere fact that they were home for the summer.

He wondered, Am I such an awful brother that I don't even want them around? What's the matter with me anymore? They're my brothers, for crying out loud.

Reasonable or not, the arrival of the twins last week had brought Jon a faint depression, a feeling of being always on the defensive. He felt as though he'd been demoted. The only real freedom from the mood came when he was riding Sun God.

He thought about Sunny as he rubbed Sade's stomach, savoring the knowledge that the horse was tied in the barn, that any minute now, as soon as the spirit moved him, he could get up from the grass and go for a ride.

He was just pulling up his legs to leave when Ernie said, "Um, I guess I've got an announcement to make."

Jon twisted around to look at him, caught by something in his voice. Aunt Jess stopped the swing, and Dad looked up. Elton was watching his brother quizzically.

"Well, what it is, Dad, I've decided not to go back to school next fall."

Elton stared. "What the . . ."

Dad flipped away his cigarette. "What did you want to do, Ernie?" His voice was even.

"Stay home. Start pulling my share of the load around here. I thought maybe we could work out the partnership arrangement that you said we would, if any of us wanted to stay on the farm. You know, a percentage of the cropland, and my hogs—all that . . ."

Jon heard plainly the breath that Dad had been holding. "Sure, Ernie. If that's what you want. There's plenty of money for college, you know. You don't have to drop out because of that."

"I know it. I just want to get started, you know. . . ."

Elton found his voice. "Whatta you mean, Ern! You *can't* not go back next fall. We had it all planned out. We were going to get an apartment—the jobs we had all lined up at the pizza place. You can't just—"

Jon stared at Elton's face, drawn by the note of hurt, of betrayal, in his voice. It made Jon suddenly uncomfortable.

"Yes, I can, buddy." Ernie spoke quietly. "And I think it's time I did."

The twins stared hard at each other until finally Elton rose and went into the house, slamming the screen behind him. Almost imperceptibly, Ernie's shoulders lifted, as though he had rid himself of an old burden.

Jon stood up. "Good for you, Ern." To Aunt Jess he said, "I'm going for a ride around the mile. Hang on to Sadie, will you, till I get out of sight?"

By the time he and Sun God were on the road, the sun was hanging just over the roof of Cal White's barn. They rode in the broad, shallow grassy ditch, because Sunny's unshod back hooves were beginning to wear low, and Jon's spending money wouldn't cover a blacksmith bill for another couple of weeks.

The heat of the day still lay close to the ground, but as they rode, a light breeze came up. It was hot air, but at least it was moving. Cal White, his sister and brother-in-law, and a few of their children were in Cal's front yard. Jon raised a hand at them.

Two of the children broke loose from the group by the house and raced across the yard to stand beside the mailbox as Jon rode by.

"Look at the horse!"

"Isn't it pretty?"

"I wish we could ride it."

The last was clearly meant for Jon to overhear, but he rode on, feeling slightly mean and slightly superior. He remembered standing by his own mailbox years ago and watching Cal's daughters jog past on their Appaloosas. The girls had long since married

93

and moved away, and the Appaloosas had disappeared, but still he remembered with painful clarity how it had felt, standing there watching them.

Beyond Cal's hayfield, he turned right on the pink-graveled mile road. After a mile, he turned right again on an almost identical road. The scenery was too flat, too familiar, to be interesting, and it began to seem as though the next mile road was never going to show up.

It did, though, and after Sun God turned onto it, heading home now, his walk lengthened into a fidgity half-trot.

"Okay, fella, let's run a while." Jon relaxed his hold on Sunny's mouth. They stayed at a controlled canter until Sun God's neck was dark and wet and beginning to suds up where the reins rubbed. Then Jon pulled him down to a trot. It wasn't easy. Sunny wanted to run, heat or no heat.

"Come on, now," Jon coaxed. "Take it easy. You'll have a stroke or something."

The sun was out of sight by now, and the details of the road ahead were blurred in twilight blue. Jon was glad to see his road coming into sight at the top of the next slight rise. His legs were tired from the long day and from holding onto Sun God's slick bare back.

As they turned onto the road going south again, the roof of home came into view above the row of windbreak trees. Jon dropped the knotted reins on

Sunny's neck to stretch his tired hands and arms. At that instant, Sun God bolted.

Jon grabbed frantically and managed to hold himself on with a double handful of mane. He recovered his reins, but they were useless. Sun God had the bit in his teeth, and the barn in his sights.

In a sweat of terror, Jon thought, Maybe this is the time, the time he throws me bad—or falls and breaks a leg—or . . .

The road flashed by, blurred by speed and darkness. Fence posts, utility poles, revolved past the corners of his eyes. Beneath him, the slick barrel of Sun God surged, pounded, threw him up and caught him.

At the mailbox, Sun God leaned into the turn at so sharp an angle that the corner of the metal box sliced high on Jon's leg, almost to the knee. He felt faint.

Up the lane they pounded. Sade appeared, barking, in front of them. Sunny swerved, clattered past the dog, flew straight toward the looming front of the barn. He slid to a halt so suddenly, so close to the barn, that gravel sprayed and ticked against the boards.

Jon saw the ridge of Sunny's neck for an instant before it cracked into his face. He threw his arms up. His right arm wrapped automatically around Sun God's neck, so that when he fell he landed on his feet, his arm still crooked over the neck.

Before he could breathe, they all came down on

him. "You crazy whelp!" Dad stormed. "What do you mean, running that horse like that, scaring us out of our wits? You know better than that!"

Ernie, closest to Jon, whispered, "You all right?" Jon nodded and turned toward Sunny's mane.

"Was he running away with you, or were you making him do that?" Aunt Jess peered at him through the dark.

"I'll tell you one thing right now, young man," Dad said. "If I ever catch you pulling a stupid trick like that again, that horse goes."

They all turned and trudged back to the house—all except Ernie, who followed Jon and Sun God into the barn. When the barn door was closed and the yellow light switched on, Ernie said, "Just how long do you think you're going to be able to fool them?"

Jon led Sunny into the stall and replaced the bridle with the halter.

"Jon, will you pay attention to me? Now, you're going to mess around and get yourself really hurt with that horse, and then Dad will make you get rid of him, and you won't stand a chance of getting another one. Why don't you use your head? Sell that thing and get one you can handle. Dad's no dummy, you know. He—"

Jon came out of the stall then, but stood with one hand still touching Sun God's thigh. His face was blotched red with fury. His voice shook.

"Ernie McBride, if you ever say one word to Dad

or anybody, I'll hate you as long as I live. Sunny's my horse. I can handle him, and I love him. And he loves . . ." His voice broke as he turned back into the stall. "Go mind your own business."

In the silence of the shadow-filled barn, Sade whimpered once from where she sat, half crouched between the boys, taking their angry voices as personal blows.

Finally Ernie sighed. "Okay, just don't say I didn't warn you. Come on, Sadie. He doesn't want you around, either."

She hesitated, looking from Ernie to Jon. Then she followed Ernie out of the barn, her tail low.

11

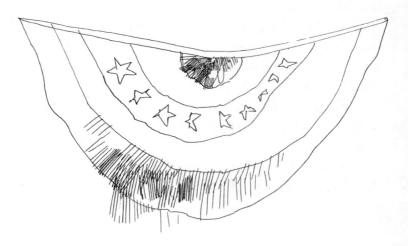

"Looks like it'll make 'knee high by the Fourth of July,' doesn't it?" Cal White knocked his pipe against the top board of the fence and squinted out across the field of corn.

Jon stood beside him, elbows and chin hooked over the gate. He was remembering last Fourth, when he and Ernie had sat on this gate in the rain and he'd wished so hard for his horse.

"Yeah. It's already way past my knees."

Cal opened his mouth to say something about Jon's knees being lower than anyone else's, but glancing at the boy, he realized Jon's eyes were no longer so very far beneath his own.

In the pasture beyond the corn, a flash of gold caught Jon's eyes, and he turned away from Cal. As he watched Sunny appear and disappear among the trees out there, he listened for Aunt Jess to come out of the house. If she'd hurry up with her getting ready, and come and take her date off his hands, he'd still have time for a ride before dark.

Cal interrupted his thoughts. "You going to ride your horse in the parade Saturday?"

Jon shifted his weight to the other leg. "I don't know yet. I thought about it." When Cal didn't answer, he went on. "I'd like to, but that old army saddle's such a wreck I don't even use it around the place anymore. I sure as heck wouldn't ride down Main Street in it."

They were quiet for a moment. On the ground between them, Sade made a vicious lunge at a flea at the base of her tail, groaning softly as she dug the spot with her teeth.

"I know what. Why don't you borrow our good black outfit? Margie wanted me to hang onto it till she and her husband get some horses, but you're sure welcome to use it for special occasions like the parade if you want."

For a fleeting instant, Jon felt trapped, but then common sense took over. "Hey, thanks. That'd be perfect. I'll take good care of it."

Cal's hand clamped his shoulder in a casual way. Then Aunt Jess came billowing down the back porch steps in her squaw dress, and Cal left.

There was daylight enough for a quick ride, but instead of going for his bridle, Jon climbed the gate and settled his seat bones as comfortably as possible on the narrow board.

Well, that settles it, he thought. I'm going to ride him in the parade. If he gets away from me or anything, well, it'll just have to happen. But maybe he won't. Maybe he'll be okay. And it would be kind of fun, riding such a beautiful horse, with all those little kids watching and wishing they were me. I know—I'll get to the parade ground plenty early, and if he acts too nervous, we can always pull out before the parade starts. It'd be mean to put him through an ordeal that was going to scare him.

As he thought about the parade, a bad taste came in his mouth, a metallic sort of taste. Like before a dental appointment. He found himself walking through the corn, between the rows, toward the pasture. The long deep-green corn leaves crisscrossed his path like a gamut of limp swords, cutting lightly at his bare arms as he pushed through. Ahead of him, a bull snake slithered into life and disappeared. By the time he reached the end of the cornfield, the bad taste was nearly gone.

He spoke out loud. "I am going to ride my beautiful horse in the parade, and I am going to control him." His stomach was tight with determination, and it stayed tight until the morning of the Fourth.

100

The components of the parade were gathering in the high school parking lot. The combined senior and junior high school bands were grouped near the school building. A flock of smaller children stood in another clump with crepe-papered bicycles, and a dozen or so convertibles with placards tied to their flanks drove slowly about the lot. Other New Hope parade stand-bys were there, too—a Jaycee clown on a donkey, three Shriners in midget autos that bucked and reared, half a dozen floats sponsored by various businesses, and a miniature covered wagon pulled by a beautifully matched six-pony hitch from Sorenson's Pony Farm.

And there were the horses. A few of the riders were Saddle Club members. They wore gold satin shirts with NHSC emblems on the backs. But most of the riders were children and teen-agers gleaned from farms, acreages, and edge-of-town pony pastures. Jon knew most of them slightly, none of them well.

As he rode toward them, he forced himself to sit easy, to take a more relaxed hold on the reins. At least I've got the best-looking outfit here, he thought grimly.

Sun God had never looked more radiant. He'd been bathed and brushed. His mane and tail had been rinsed in bluing. His fetlocks were trimmed to the bone. His golden coat stood out in sharp contrast to the black of Cal White's rig.

The saddle was huge, with white padded seat and black-and-white-striped corona outlining it. The stirrup tapaderos curved gracefully to Sun God's knees. The matching breastplate seemed to accentuate the powerful mold of the horse's chest, and the four huge silver conchos hanging in a heavy line down the center of Sun God's head, from browband to noseband, glittered with every move. Jon wore his newest wheat-colored Levis, a western shirt of soft green plaid with pearl snaps, and the boots he wore so seldom for fear of scarring their tan rough-out leather.

The band began to warm up as Jon reached the other riders. He raised his hand in brief greeting, then turned his attention to Sun God.

The horse stiffened at the first blatting noise of the band. He lifted his head as high as he could and stared across the field at the sun glaring off of a tuba. He stood still, but Jon could feel the tension coming through the reins.

The bulk of the saddle seemed to separate him from Sunny. He felt high up, out of touch. And the saddle horn got in the way of his rein hand. The stirrups were a little too long, also, but there hadn't been time to adjust them at Cal's this morning, when he stopped to get the saddle, and he didn't want to get off now to do it.

By the time the elements of the parade had been marshalled into place, some of the tension had left Sun God. Jon began to think he and Sunny might make it through all right, after all. He took his place beside a young girl on a placid brown mare, and waited for the command to march.

The band began to play, and a few minutes later the horse in front of Sun God moved off. Once they were under way, Jon's apprehension began to ease. Although the narrow street's curbs were packed solid with shouting, waving people, and the band music was shrill, and all the elements that would ordinarily frighten a horse were there, Sun God clacked along the blacktopped street as steadily as a veteran parade horse. He arched his neck, swiveled his ears, rolled his eyes toward the crowd, lifted his hooves much higher than was necessary. Still he stayed in line and moved with the others.

By the time they had left Vine Street for the brick-paved downtown square, Jon was riding high and easy, genuinely smiling at the people they passed, basking in the beauty that Sun God reflected.

The parade disintegrated in the Legion Park a few blocks north of the square. It was a densely shaded park, a block square, with the library in one corner and a bandstand in the center.

Jon reined Sunny up close to a tree, out of the main course of traffic, to watch for the twins. While he waited, he glanced casually over the crowd. He felt vaguely disappointed when no one from his class at school appeared, but in a matter of minutes there was a gratifying number of small children staring at Sun God.

One boy pushed his way to the front. "Hey,

could I ride your horse?" he asked.

Jon smiled and shook his head. He felt taller than he ever had before. "Sorry, but he's a one-man horse. Nobody but me can handle him."

Then Ernie was there. "You want to take Sunny home now? I'll follow you in the car and bring you back, if you want."

For a moment, Jon wavered. It was good, being up on Sun God with all these people around. But on second thought, he realized it would be no small relief to have Sunny safely home, in spite of the horse's surprisingly good behavior. "Okay, but give me a good long head start, will you?"

The two-mile ride home was much pleasanter than the ride into town a few hours earlier. Sun God loped along the shallow ditches, and Jon sang cowboy songs and twirled the ends of the reins like a lariat.

Aloud, he was singing the songs' well-known lyrics, but on a deeper level, he sang a private song. I rode you, Sun God. I handled you.

For the first time, he felt deeply sure that Sun God was his horse.

Home was in sight by the time Ernie slowed the convertible beside him. Jon raised his hand to wave. Sun God exploded beneath him. They were galloping full out. The gently prancing horse who had behaved so beautifully through the terror of the parade was bolting for home, neck stretched level with the ground, ears flattened.

104

Jon regained his balance as best he could. He hauled on the reins, but he knew with a sinking stomach that he couldn't reach Sunny. The hot air pushed against his face. The road and the fence posts revolved past. His legs grew weak in their grip.

It was an old nightmare. Fleetingly he knew what was coming—the dizzy fall, the jar when he hit the ground, maybe worse. He didn't care. Something inside him gave up.

At the lane, Sunny swerved as only Sunny could. Jon hung in the air, suspended by the hand that grabbed at random and fastened around the saddle horn. Then, with a bucking kick, Sun God swerved away from him, and Jon sailed, crashed, skidded on his shoulder and back across the cinder lane.

He wanted to lie there forever, at the bottom of his misery, knowing it was going to be worse in a minute when his shoulder and his thoughts caught up with him. But Sade had come, nosing at his face, whining softly in his ear, wanting to play. He rolled over on his stomach. The urge to cry swelled painfully inside him, crowding his lungs, constricting his throat. One hand began savagely ripping up the grass.

Then Ernie's knee was beside his face. "Are you all right? Is anything broken, do you think? Jon? Can you get up?"

The shakiness in Ernie's voice penetrated Jon's fury. He sat up.

"I'm okay. Just knocked the wind out of me, I

guess. Listen, would you unsaddle Sunny and turn him out, while I go change my shirt?"

Together they turned toward the barn. Sun God was grazing peacefully just outside the lot fence.

"You sure you're okay? Nothing busted?"

"Nothing busted." But he avoided looking at his horse as he walked toward the house.

When Ernie came up to the bathroom a few minutes later, Jon was standing with his back to the mirror, looking over his shoulder at the reflection. His right shoulder blade was scraped clean of skin, and burned-looking areas extended down and across his back as far as his belt. Small bits of cinder were embedded here and there like paprika on a breast of chicken.

Ernie whistled softly. He made a close, grimacing inspection of the raw back, then reached into the medicine cabinet for the iodine.

"Don't put anything on it," Jon snapped. "But would you mind just kind of washing it off with cold water and getting out the rocks?"

He sat on the edge of the bathtub and gripped its porcelain rim while Ernie went to work with washcloth and tweezers on his back. They were silent until the job was done.

Then Ernie said, "Okay, buddy, but I think you ought to have some iodine or something on that. And I'll be very curious to see how you explain this to Dad and Aunt Jess."

Jon smiled at the soap dish. It wasn't a happy smile, but a wise one, a rather cool one.

Riding back to town with clean hands and face, a clean shirt and a burning back, Jon noticed the small flag that waved from the car's hood ornament.

"Hey. That's it, I bet."

Ernie looked at him.

He motioned at the flag. "I bet that flag was what scared Sunny. When you came up beside us, he probably saw that flag flapping in the breeze and . . ." Under Ernie's gaze, his voice faltered.

Ernie spoke deliberately, as though Jon were a very young child. "If that horse made it through the parade, brother Jon, without spooking at anything, I find it hard to believe a little six-inch paper flag would scare him into running away with you. When are you going to wise up to him?"

They rode the rest of the way in cold silence.

12

Jon spent the afternoon avoiding his family. It wasn't hard. Although the Legion Park was small, the Jaycees had turned it into a carnival midway that had attracted most of the county's population.

Sorenson's Pony Farm had roped off a small corral and was selling pony rides for a quarter. There was a pitch-the-coin-in-the-saucer booth, a weight-guessing stand, and a booth where, for a quarter, you could toss a baseball and dunk a Jaycee member into a water trough.

At the bandstand, a talent contest was under way. Jon saw Dad and Aunt Jess in the crowd around the stand. He waved to let them know he was back, but ducked away before they could invite him to join them.

Although he wasn't hungry, he bought a runny beefburger and a bottle of pop, and made his way around the park, eating as he went.

After a while, Aunt Jess appeared out of the crowd. "Jon, we're about ready to go home. You want to come?"

He swallowed the last of the beefburger before he answered her. "No, I'm going to get in the greased-pig contest. I can ride back with the twins or somebody if you guys want to go on."

She looked at him quizzically, but didn't question him. "Well, if you're going to be in a contest, Dad and I'll wait around and watch. I think they're getting ready for it now. You better get over there."

He found a trash can for the remains of his lunch, and loped through the crowd toward the arena. It was a small roughly oval enclosure made of wavering snow fence. He gave his name and age to the man with the notebook who guarded the break in the fence, and then slipped inside.

The dozen or so boys inside the arena had removed their shirts. Jon glanced at the chairs outside the fence, spotted Aunt Jess, and left his shirt on. Along with the others, he was herded into one corner of the arena and held there by the outstretched arms of a grinning Jaycee member. He could feel the tension that came off the other boys in waves, but it rolled over him without touching him. He allowed himself to be elbowed back into the fence.

In the opposite corner of the arena, a large rust-colored oil drum was lowered to the ground and tipped over. A furious, half-grown Poland China emerged at a run. The Jaycee dropped his arms.

The pig squealed and reversed in his tracks, but the pack of boys charged, bare arms flailing, denim-wrapped legs churning. Jon was in the middle of the pack when someone made a flying tackle. Bodies fell; knees and elbows waved. Jon's legs were knocked back. His face was shoved into someone's ribs near the ground. A foot came down for an instant on the tip of his nose. There were bodies on top of him, grinding him down. He smiled grimly.

When the heap had sorted itself out and climbed to its collective feet, Jon saw the pig dangling by one hind leg from the hand of a boy too small or too timid to have been in the melee. He slapped at the dust on his pants and wiped at his face with his shirt sleeve. Aunt Jess was waiting at the gate.

"Okay, Aunt Jess, if you want to go home now, I'm ready."

As soon as they got home, Aunt Jess demanded his shirt. "Look at that. Tore the pocket off, all but a thread, and look at this tear in the back. This shirt hasn't been worn more than a . . . Good grief, boy, your back looks like a beefsteak."

She turned him, none too gently, toward the

light. "Why, you've skinned your whole back raw, Jon. That's the worst-looking thing I've ever seen. Elton, Ernie, somebody, go get me the iodine, will you?" She prodded the edges of the scrapes carefully with her thumb.

Quietly Sade stood up against Jon, her front legs against his bare chest, her eyes watching his. At the first touch of the cool glass rod with its burning iodine, his fists tightened in the long hair at her throat.

"Honest to goodness, Jon McBride, this is the last greased-pig chase for you. You don't have sense enough to take off your good shirt, and you not only tear up the shirt, you break every bone in your body."

"It would be the last time anyway," he said complacently. "Next year I'll be too old."

". . . hasn't got the sense God gave a goat," she muttered.

A few days later they began the second cutting of the field of timothy hay across the pasture lane from the cornfield.

As he guided the mower through the pale green hay, the sun bit deep into Jon's shoulders and seared the small new scabs on his bare back. The air moved in humid waves before his eyes. He wanted to close his eyes to the dizziness of it, and just breathe in the thick warm-sun smell that followed the swish of the blades through the feathery hay.

He felt curiously good, in spite of the fact that

sweat and chaff were making his back almost unbearably itchy. Even the heat seemed less a discomfort than a challenge, as he made his slow rounds of the field. Nature or God or whatever it was, was pressing down its worst on him, and he withstood.

"Hundred and three," Dad commented, as they met at the fence to share a thermos of cold water. They smiled at each other, sweat pouring from their scalps and dripping from their noses.

He felt close to Dad. They were standing together against the elements.

At breakfast on the day after the mowing was done, Elton said, "We going to rake today, Dad?"

Dad stopped working his mouthful of scrambled egg, picked a bit of eggshell from his tongue, and said, "Nope."

"We better, hadn't we?"

Jon stopped eating and looked at Elton. Is it just my imagination, he wondered, or is Elton getting kind of mouthy with Dad these days?

It seemed to him that ever since Ernie had decided to stay home and farm, Elton hadn't missed a chance to show off his knowledge of how the farm should be run. Jon wondered if Elton was afraid Ernie would get the inside track with Dad, while he was away in college.

"Nope," Dad repeated. "Better to leave it lay another day or so."

"It's going to get too dry," Elton warned. "That sun's hot."

"Do tell."

"The leaves'll come off if you wait too long."

Jon cringed inwardly at Elton's tone. You could only push Dad so far.

"Is that what you learned at engineering college? Since you're so smart, how come you're forgetting the minor fact the humidity is in the high nineties? Huh, college boy? That hay needs another day curing, and I'll thank you not to try telling me how to run this place. Not for a few years yet!"

They finished breakfast in silence, and the hay was left to cure another day in the field.

On his way down the pasture lane to get Sun God, Jon stopped for a minute beside a fence post and dropped the bridle. The hayfield, the fragrance and the pattern of it, held him. Long windrows of hay stretched away in easy waves, following the contour of the gently rolling field like green-gold corduroy.

He began thinking how much fun it would be to gallop across there, jumping the windrows. Sunny could jump them easily. They were long soft humps of hay, no more than three feet wide and a couple of feet high, spaced ten or twelve feet apart. It would be simple.

Sun God was near the gate, with a handful of calves. As Jon opened the gate, Sade left him and bounded over the long grass toward her calves. Hiding the bridle behind him and offering the ear of corn, Jon approached. He stopped and waited as Sunny moved toward him.

Watching the horse, aching at the beauty of him, Jon imagined there was no ear of corn for bait, that Sunny was coming to him out of affection. Then, with a snort of cynicism, he told himself, "Come on, stupid. Be realistic. It's the corn he's coming to, and you know it."

In the hayfield, he rode Sunny up to the first windrow for a look. Then, getting a good handful of mane, he put his heels into Sunny's ribs. The horse gathered himself and hopped over the hay.

Jon slapped him on the neck. "Good boy. That's the way. Now we'll do it right."

All he knew about jumping was the little he'd read in horse books, but instinctively he knew he could do it. He set Sun God in a canter down the field between the windrows. Then, catching his breath, he reined to the right.

The jump was hardly more than an extension of Sun God's canter, and the landing was smooth. Before Jon had a chance to feel elated, the second windrow, the second leap, came and went.

Across the field they sailed, a few cantering beats, a pause, a lifting, then the cantering resumed. A feeling of weightlessness, of restrained power, flowed through Jon. He burned with a happiness so intense that its fading was a relief.

At the far fence, he pulled Sunny up and let him cool off before they started back. When he looked over the way they had come, he saw Sade loping toward them around the edge of the field by the pasture. Her tongue was lolling, her head low. She dropped to the grass beside Sun God, panting heavily.

"Sadie, you're going to have a heart attack some-day doing that. Why don't you go on back to the house, where it's cool?"

She grinned up at him and wagged. Sun God flicked back his ears and sidled away from her.

"Okay, fella. I guess you're cooled off enough. Let's jump them going back now."

Sunny sailed over the first three windrows. At the fourth, abruptly, he balked. Jon somersaulted over Sunny's lowered head, over the hay. The ground and sky revolved lazily before his eyes. He almost didn't care.

Then the ground came up to meet his back. The short stiff hay stubble pierced his still-raw skin. For an instant, his breath was gone, and the sky went black.

When he got up, Sun God was tearing huge mouthfuls of hay from the top of the windrow. For the first time, Jon approached his horse with a feeling that he was going into battle.

13

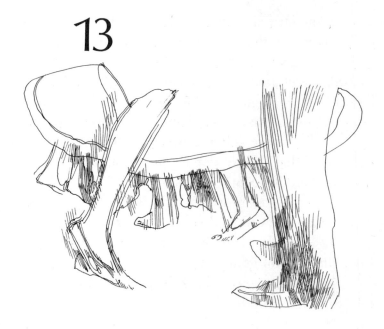

"I think we should bale today." Elton looked at Dad, his face hardened with belligerence.

They were at breakfast—and at war—again.

Jon opened his mouth to say "Don't teach your grandmother to suck eggs," but after looking from Elton to Dad, he decided to stay out of it.

"It needs another day," Dad said around a mouthful of toast. "It's too green yet."

A familiar bulldog expression settled on Elton's face. He's arguing for the fun of it now, Jon thought.

"What if it rains tonight? The forecast said possible showers. Would you rather have it a shade too green, or wet and moldy?"

Dad gave him a hard stare. "We'll bale to-morrow."

"I think we ought to do it today."

Dad's fork hit the table in a spatter of egg. He surged up, tipping over his chair. His face was angry red as he bellowed, "All right! You're so smart, go ahead and bale. I don't know anything about it. I've only been running this place twenty-five years. I'll be damned if I'm going to sit here and argue about it. Young whelps . . ." He left the table, muttering, and slammed through the screen door.

The kitchen echoed silence, except for the tick of forks as those around the table resumed eating. Dad's fury, so seldom directed at one of the twins, left an atmosphere that subdued even Elton. Sade was plastered, trembling, against Jon's leg under the table.

But Elton wasn't so subdued as to relinquish his victory. The three boys baled. All through that day and the next, Jon and the twins worked in the hayfield, while Dad found things that needed doing in other parts of the farm. Between the three of them, the long windrows of hay were swept up into the baling machine, discharged in compact twine-wrapped blocks, loaded on racks, and hoisted by the forklift through the huge hayloft window in the front of the barn. Toward the end of the second day, it seemed to Jon that he'd been doing this since the beginning of time.

He and Elton were in the loft, stacking the bales, while Ernie worked the forklift on the ground outside.

The air in the loft was stifling. Dust and chaff rose in clouds as Jon dropped his bale onto the stack against the wall. His work gloves were wet with sweat, but he knew if he took them off, the baling twine would blister his hands.

He went to the loft window and yelled down to Ernie, "How about trading jobs for a while? You get all the breeze."

Ernie's wiry black hair, his bare red back and shoulders, were dusted with chaff. He didn't bother to look up. "We don't have very much to do yet. You can stand it. This is the last load."

Jon looked at the nearly full hayrack, estimated a good thirty bales yet to go, and sighed as he withdrew.

Elton was getting tired of the job, too. Jon noticed he was tossing the bales on top of one another as though he didn't care where they landed. As Jon debated whether or not to make an issue of stacking them straight and tight, as they were supposed to, he heard a car door slam below.

"Probably an insurance salesman," Elton said, so loudly that his voice could well have reached the car outside. Jon frowned at him.

"Hey, Jon." Ernie's voice came up through the window. "There's a man here to see you."

He was a large man, nearly bald, with a heavy-jowled face. He'd taken off his suit jacket, turned back his shirt cuffs, and removed his tie, but even so he gave the appearance of being well groomed.

"Howdy there, I'm Jack Whitaker, Whitaker Ford Agency over at Boone." He shook Jon's hand and gave him a business card.

Jon took the card and the handshake and waited for an explanation. Surely he didn't come out here to sell me a car, he thought.

"Understand you've got a horse I used to own. I was in the neighborhood, thought I'd stop in and take a look at him, see if it's the same one. Big dark palomino gelding?"

"Oh. Sure." Jon grinned, then turned to the twins. "You guys go ahead without me." He tried not to look smugly at Elton.

As they started down the pasture lane, Mr. Whitaker said, "Fellow I know here in town saw you riding Prince in the Fourth of July parade. Happened to mention it to me the other day. He knew I'd always been crazy about that horse. I raised him from a colt, you know. Broke him myself. Here a few years ago, my wife had a bad spell, spent about a year at the clinic up in Rochester. I sold most all my horses, and there wasn't a one I regretted losing more than I did Prince."

Jon walked a little slower, suddenly afraid of how Sunny might react to this man, afraid the affection he'd been watching for so eagerly would show itself now—for the man who had raised him from a colt.

Sun God lifted his head and watched them come toward him through the long meadow grass. He stopped chewing and waited, with a look of distrust about him, as Jon came up slowly and caught his halter. With Jon and Mr. Whitaker standing on either side of his head, Sun God turned to Jon and lipped his shirt front.

Inaudibly Jon sighed. *He turned to me.*

Mr. Whitaker ran a hand over Sunny's neck. "Hey there, old Prince. How ya doing, boy? You look like they been taking good care of you."

He smiled across the horse's neck at Jon. Jon smiled back, a huge generous smile.

The man walked once around Sun God, studying him. "Wish I'd worn my other clothes. I'd have liked to give him a try."

"You can come back some other time and ride him if you want," Jon offered.

"That's about as easy-gaited a horse as I ever rode. I used to show him in western pleasure a lot. Got a bundle of ribbons at home that he won me."

They were quiet for a few minutes. Jon toyed with Sunny's forelock, laying it straight and even down the center of his head. He wished Sun God would nuzzle him again while the man was watching.

"Don't suppose you'd care to sell him?"

Jon started. He looked around Sunny's head and met Mr. Whitaker's gaze. "Not a chance." He put an arm around Sunny's neck and pulled it close. "I'm pretty attached to this horse."

The man grinned, shrugged, turned back toward the barn. Halfway back he said, "Tell you what. I'll give you two-fifty for him as he stands. How does that strike you?"

Jon tried not to let his pleasure show. Of course it was out of the question, but it was a great feeling, knowing someone wanted his horse two hundred and fifty dollars worth. It was proof positive he'd made a good buy, that Sun God was a good horse in someone's eyes other than his own. He could hardly wait to tell the rest of the family.

"That's a good offer, Mr. Whitaker, and I appreciate it. But I couldn't get along without that horse."

Back at the car, they shook hands again.

"You hang onto my card anyway, and if you should change your mind, the offer stands."

Jon smiled, nodded, waved him off.

In the loft window overhead, Elton and Ernie appeared. From where Jon stood, they looked like denim-clad, hairy-chested giants. Pale green chaff from the hay covered both of them.

Jon grinned up. "Ho, ho, ho, jolly green giants," he said before he thought. He felt good.

"What was all that about?" Ernie motioned toward the car disappearing down the lane.

"Guy that used to own Sun God." Jon squinted up at them. "He heard I had him, and came to try and get him back. He offered me two hundred and fifty dollars for him." Carefully he kept his voice casual.

"*Sure* he did," Elton said as he disappeared from the window.

"Did he really?" Ernie asked.

Jon nodded, pride shining from his face.

"I suppose you turned it down."

"Well, of course I turned it down. What would I want to sell Sunny for?"

"I think you're crazy." Ernie disappeared from the window, too.

At the supper table the following Friday, Aunt Jess suggested that the family might enjoy coming to the square dance with her and Cal that night.

"Might as well," Jon said. "There's nothing good on television."

Dad agreed it sounded all right to him.

"We've both got dates," Elton said. "And by the way, Ernie, dibs on the convertible."

Ernie gave him a long cold look, but said, "Can I use your car, Dad?" Dad nodded. "Thanks."

Aunt Jess seemed so pleased that at least part of her family was coming to watch her dance that Jon felt vaguely uncomfortable, as though it was something he should have thought of himself a long time ago.

The Elks' Hall, where the Allemande Leftovers

met, was upstairs over the First National Bank, on the west side of the square in New Hope. Cal White parked in front of the bank, and Jon followed the others across the sidewalk toward the entrance, suddenly conscious of the stifling weight of the air. It had been one of the hottest days of the year, and now there was an oppressive hint of a storm coming.

"The Elks' is air-conditioned, I hope," Dad puffed as they climbed the wide, dark stairway that separated the bank from the shoe store.

"You bet," Aunt Jess said. "If it wasn't, us old folks would all be dead of heart attacks by now."

The hall, at the top of the stairs and to the left, was brightly lit, a large square room, bare of furniture except for a grand piano in one corner and folding chairs along the walls. Across the front of the room, high windows looked out on the town square. A long serving window in the wall at the back opened onto a kitchen.

Dad and Jon sat alone in the folding chairs near the door, while Aunt Jess and Cal joined the other dancers. Some twenty people were moving about the room—middle-aged husbands and wives in their square-dance outfits: western shirts, boots, and string ties for the men; full-skirted peasant or squaw dresses, many with matching bloomers, for the women. Each wore a black "Allemande Leftovers" pin, and every face was smiling.

Jon recognized most of them, although he

couldn't put names to very many. Several of the couples were parents of his classmates. They were about half town and half farm people, he judged, counting the number of men with weathered faces and pale foreheads.

In the far corner, a man who was evidently the caller fiddled with an impressive-looking turntable and microphone set that rested on the piano. He was fairly young, black-haired and outdoorsy-looking, and he did a little dance step as he thumbed through a metal file box of records. Finally he found one, set it on the turntable, and faced the room, snapping the cord of the throat mike around his neck.

"All right, folks, I think we've got enough for two squares now, so if you'll form your sets, we'll start off with a little 'Kansas City Gal.'"

The kaleidoscope of men and women divided itself into two squares of four couples each, holding hands and smiling at one another in anticipation. Aunt Jess and Cal were in the square nearest Jon. She glanced back at him and Dad to make sure they were watching.

Somewhat to Jon's surprise, he realized she didn't look at all out of place there, with her gray hair and full-skirted dress. Several of the women appeared to be about her age or older, and most of the men were graying or balding or both.

The music started. The dancers swung their clasped hands and bounced on the balls of their feet as the rhythm made itself felt.

The caller sang out. "All join hands and circle to the left. Swing your corner with your ole left hand, back to your partner with a right-and-left grand."

Jon's foot moved with the rhythm.

"Now trot that gal around the tcwn, big foot up an' little foot down. Head couples split the ring—go 'round two, make a line of four. . . . *Swing* through, *star* through. Take that pretty gal home with you. . . ."

The fiddle, guitar, and bass music was no less intriguing for being recorded. Jon found his leg pumping in time to it. He got up, swung his chair around backwards, and sat down again, straddling it.

"Box the gnat and pull her by. Box the flea, I don't know why. . . . Circle to the left till the break of day. Now roll away with a half-sashay.

"Bow to your corners, partners, all. Wave to the purty gal 'cross the hall. No more, folks. That's it; that's all."

As the dances followed one another, with just short rests between, Jon studied the calls, the patterns, the rules of the game. He began to feel as though he could do it himself if he had a chance.

As the sets were being squared after one of the breaks, a man in Aunt Jess's square looked over his shoulder at Dad, glanced down at his wife beside him, then back at Dad. "Hey, John. How about taking over for me on this next one? I can't get the old lady to quit, and I'm about stomped into the floor."

His wife, a rubber ball of a woman in a red gingham dress, made a face at him. "I'm after your insurance, big boy. Come on, John. I'll out-dance the both of you."

Dad shook his head, grinned uncomfortably, but finally allowed himself to be pulled into the square. Jon settled back in his seat, disappointed. He'd been on the verge of volunteering himself.

As the dance got under way, he realized that Dad was no stranger to this. He was a little hesitant, but with the guidance of the others in the square, he managed to find his way through what seemed to Jon an intricate pattern of movements.

Maybe he and Mother used to square dance, Jon mused. The thought was disturbing.

"Head couple pass through, cross-trail, go 'round two to a line of four. Bend the line and swing once more, swing old mother off the floor."

Dad threw back his head. A huge silent laugh split his face as he wrapped his arms about his little round partner and whirled her through the air. One small red shoe left her foot and sailed across the floor. Through the laughter that filled the room, the kitchen telephone rang.

"Promenade around the town, big foot up, little foot down!"

The kitchen door opened, and the caller's wife, a tray of ice cubes in one hand and the phone in the other, shrilled, "John McBride! Your barn's on fire!"

14

It was a hellish ride.

Cal ran red lights all around the square, nearly hitting a girl at one intersection. Outside of town the Buick barreled through the dark, outrunning the headlights, sluing curves, throwing gravel against its underside.

Jon sat in front. His clenched fist beat on the dashboard. His forehead nearly touched the windshield. His mouth hung slack. Anguish twisted his face.

Sunny, Sunny, Sunny, Sunny, he screamed silently. Before his eyes, sickening him, hypnotizing him, was the sight of Sun God tied in his stall, fight-

127

ing the rope, smothering in smoke—touched by flames. . . .

The Buick lashed around a curve and thundered across Walnut Creek bridge. Another curve and they could see, ahead and to the right, a low red cloud of smoke rising to lose itself in the lowering storm clouds.

"Thank God the steers are—out. . . ." Dad's voice faded at the picture of forty-three terrified young steers penned in the small, tightly fenced lot bordered on one side by the burning barn, on three sides by barbed wire.

They were racing the length of the cornfield now. Over the head-high corn, they could see the silhouette of the barn.

It's not happening, Jon thought. It's not . . .

The barn, the largest building on the farm, was etched against the sky as they jounced into the lane. Stark black it stood, the nucleus, the focal point, the heart of the farm, its windows solid squares of orange. Spears of flame pierced the roof and poured out the loft door. The entire wall nearest them, where the door was, was a sheet of flame.

Jon didn't know whether the roaring came from the fire or his head. Sunny, Sunny, oh my God, don't let him . . .

He flew across the grass toward the lot fence, unaware that he stumbled, fell, got up again. Dimly he felt the ocean of heat through which he moved. It enveloped him, pushed him down and back, dragged at his legs. He seemed to be moving in slow motion through this dream, toward the fence that wavered, rippled, moved away as he tried to overtake it.

Finally the hot rough boards of it were in his grasp. He pulled himself up and over. As he floated down on the other side, a streak of white crossed his vision from right to left.

The barn door was there, close now. Part of his mind heard and registered the sound of hooves crashing, crashing against wood. The door was wavering. The wall around it swam. Through the wisps of smoke, he saw the white form fling itself against the door. It fell back, wailing.

The heat was shrinking his skin. Something more than the heat was holding him back. It had him by the arms. Furiously he thrashed against it.

Then the white shape flung itself again. This time the door exploded outward, and Sun God leaped away. As he thundered past, Jon's mind photographed indelibly the scarlet lining of the flared nostrils; the huge eye, reflecting red, that didn't see him; the golden shoulder hairs, standing out from the skin, tipped in black, trailing miniature wisps of smoke.

The last thing he saw was the lump of Sade, lying near the gaping door.

When things came into focus again, he was lying on the davenport in the brightly lit living room. The face of a strange man loomed close. Behind it hovered Aunt Jess.

"There he comes now," the fireman said. "Didn't I tell you it was just a little smoke in the lungs? A whiff of oxygen and he's good as new. But let me warn you, my boy, don't be takin' up cigarettes. You haven't got the constitution for it." He chuckled and stood up.

As the man slammed through the front door, Jon sat up. The room tilted, but quickly settled itself. Aunt Jess sat beside him.

"You can relax, Jonnie. Sun God's fine. Got a little singed here and there, and he's got a scraped leg, but he's going to be fine."

The nightmare was over. Waves of giddiness engulfed him. It was all over—all right. . . . He let his head fall back against the davenport.

"Don't you want to know about your dog?" There was an edge to Aunt Jess's voice that caught his attention. Remorse hit him. Sade! Out there, opening the barn door for Sunny! Lying out there . . .

"What happened to her!"

"Well, she's at least got a broken hind leg, maybe more. Sunny must have stepped on her as he came out. The vet's looking at her in the kitchen. I guess she thought you were in the barn, too."

Sade was stretched out on the kitchen table. Dr. Knapp stood beside her, moving her hind leg carefully back and forth. It bent in a place where it shouldn't have. On the other side of the table, Ernie stood looking down at her with tears pushing through the soot on his face.

Seeing Ernie's tears, Jon's eyes watered, too. "How is she?" he whispered.

Dr. Knapp began wrapping the still form in a small rag rug. "Right now she's in shock. The leg seems to be a clean enough break. She tore off a toe-nail on the barn door. Any internal injuries we won't know about till tomorrow or later. I'll take her back to the clinic with me now. If you want to ride along, you're welcome. I'll be coming back to check the calves."

For a moment, Jon hesitated, looking down at the white head, the brown ears, the glazed eyes that stared but didn't see. Then he thought of Sun God and the terror he must still be feeling.

"I've got to see about my horse. He was in the barn." Suddenly he leaned close to Sade and whispered, "Thank you for saving him." His throat felt swollen and aching. He avoided the others and went outside.

Two fire trucks stood in the side yard. He paused for a moment to watch the men aiming streams of water over the corncrib and the other small nearby buildings. Then he became aware of the people. The lane was parked solid with cars all the way to the road. A short round woman in a red gingham square-dance dress, Dad's dancing partner, came to stand beside Aunt Jess. Her arm stretched up around Aunt Jess's shoulders. Her small hand patted and patted.

From where he stood, on the slight rise of the side yard, Jon could see the calves bunched together at the far end of the lane. They seemed to be packed against the pasture gate, watching the fire and lowing uneasily. Silhouetted against them was the tall pale shape of Sun God. He was staring, high-headed, toward the fire, too, but just as Jon was about to start around the crowd toward him, the horse lowered his head and nervously tore up a mouthful of grass.

Suddenly it seemed too far to go, too much effort. He sank down on the back steps. When he propped his elbows on his knees, he found his arms were trembling.

"I kind of wish I'd gone in with Doc Knapp," he said, to no one in particular.

The sun warmed Jon's eyelids and woke him. He could tell from the angle of it, and from the lightness of the patch of sky he could see without moving, that it was early. The vague something-wrong feeling that had been with him even before he opened his eyes suddenly clarified. The barn. It should have kept the sun away from his window until much later.

Something else was wrong, too. He moved his legs in a sweep that covered the width of the bed. There was no heavy, warm dog stretched out across the foot of it, cramping his legs. He threw back the sheet and reached for his Levis.

First I'll go have a good look at Sunny, he thought. Then I'll see if Ernie or somebody'll take me in town to see how Sade's making out.

He worked his T-shirt down over his head, then went to the window. Even though he was expecting it, the sight of the mammoth black rectangle on the ground, the clear view of hayfield and horizon that should have been blocked off by the barn, shocked him.

He looked down into the yard and saw Dad standing looking at the charred pile. His hands were stuffed deep into his overalls. His shoulders seemed to sag, or maybe it was just the angle from which Jon saw him.

He went downstairs and through the silent house to the yard. It had rained during the night, and the grass was soaked. A few blackened beams rose from the wreckage of the barn, standing starkly against the pale early morning sky.

Dad glanced down as Jon came up beside him. Wordlessly they looked at the ruins.

"I think we got some orphans," Dad said finally. Two very young kittens were weaving toward them, crying plaintively.

Jon nodded, then turned abruptly to look away from Dad and crossed the yard toward the pasture lane.

The calves were grazing quietly along the banks

of the lane, held in by the fences on either side and the gates at each end. But not Sun God. When Jon got to the end of the lane, he found only the evidence —two splintered notches on the top edge of the gate, and the churned turf on the far side, where Sun God's hooves had landed. Far out in the pasture, there was a flash of gold through the trees that followed the creek bank.

He sighed heavily as he opened the gate. For the first time, it occurred to him that he had no bridle or grooming equipment or even halter ropes with which to ride Sunny. And no stall to tie him in to save himself the trouble of running Sun God down every time he wanted to ride.

As he began trudging through the knee-high, soaking wet pasture grass, he thought about Sunny galloping toward that high gate, gathering himself, sailing over.

Boy, I wish I could have seen that! he thought. I wish I'd been on him. He snorted. If I had, I'd have fallen off.

Sunny wasn't in a mood to be caught when Jon finally found him, especially since there was no corn in the bargain. But he did let Jon come close enough to see that the few singes and scrapes he had were minor.

"Maybe a little gentian violet on that knee," Jon murmured. "I'll pick up some at the vet's when we go in today. Okay, fella, I guess you can stay in the pasture, not that I have any choice, of course."

By the time he got back to the house, the rest of the family were eating breakfast. He stepped out of his loafers, peeled off his wet socks, and sat down.

". . . not nearly as bad as it might have been," Dad was saying. "Thank goodness Sadie let the calves out into the lane, or they'd have got smoked to death or trampled to death or gone through the barbed wire, one or the other. And there really wasn't too much of value in the barn, except the hay. Little bit of miscellaneous machinery and a lot of junk. Insurance ought to cover it all with no problems."

No one asked the question that hung in the air like smoke. What started the fire? But Jon noticed Elton said nothing more than, "Please pass the salt," all through breakfast.

After they'd eaten, Jon and Ernie drove in to Dr. Knapp's pet hospital. Sade lay unconscious in a large cage in the back room. One hind leg was enclosed in a plaster cast. A front paw was bandaged, and much of her fine white coat was singed. The shortened brown-tipped hairs stood out from her sides so that the pink skin showed through.

"Aside from the broken back leg and the torn nail," Dr. Knapp said, "she has a hairline crack in her pelvis, but no other injuries that I've been able to find. I put in a couple of stitches where she tore off the nail, and I set the leg just a little bit ago. She should be able to go home in a week or so."

Jon was a little surprised at the intensity of the relief he felt. Sade had become such an unobtrusive part of his life lately.

Politely he and Ernie looked at the X rays of Sade's leg and pelvis. But the antiseptic smell of the place began to get to him. He bought the bottle of gentian violet for Sunny's knee. and urged Ernie out to the car.

He spent the rest of the morning and much of the afternoon braiding a rope, seven feet long, from baling twine he found in the machine shed. Each strand of the braid was several twines thick, and on either end of the braid, he fastened a harness snap. The finished product was strong and smooth and not unattractive.

"There now," he said proudly. "Hook that on either side of Sunny's halter, and I've got me a perfectly good pair of reins."

While he was braiding his rope, two investigators from the insurance company had been tramping around and through the ruins of the barn with Dad, picking and kicking and peering. Jon glanced at them from time to time, but he felt no desire to leave his seat on the back steps and go over there. He didn't want to hear the verdict.

The verdict came, anyway, at the supper table. "Green hay."

At Dad's words, Jon glanced up from his plate to Dad's face, to Aunt Jess's, to Elton's. Dad's was im-

136

passive, Aunt Jess's apprehensive. Elton kept his eyes down. His fork was under the peas, but he didn't lift it to his mouth. Elton—in such a hurry to get the hay baled—to prove a point to Dad. Elton—carelessly dumping those last bales in a loose pyramid in the barn loft, a pyramid that trapped the air while the too-green hay, packed tight in its bales, heated. Of course, the extra-hot, extra-humid weather wasn't Elton's fault, but still . . .

In tense silence, they waited. Jon felt an overwhelming urge to scratch his nose, but he was afraid the movement might set off the explosion.

The silence grew. Jon tried not to think of some of the things Dad had said to *him*, for sins that were laughably small beside the grave sin of responsibility for the barn fire.

Dad spoke. "Are you boys going to pass the dumplings today or next week?"

No more was said about the fire. Jon couldn't help wondering, though, If it'd been me instead of Elton, what would Dad have done?

15

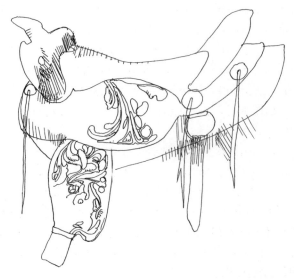

Literally before the smoke had cleared, plans for the new barn were in the blueprint stage. The contractor came on the heels of the insurance adjuster, and on Thursday evening, the blueprints were unrolled on the dining room table, their corners held down by salt and pepper shakers, a sugar bowl, and a bud vase.

Jon, Ernie, and Aunt Jess studied the plans with interest. Only Elton stayed in the living room.

The new barn would be quite a bit smaller, Jon realized as he studied the dimensions. Like the old one, it would be two stories high in the center, with single-story wings on the east and west sides. The west wing was designed for small implement storage, the center room for general storage and work space, and the east wing for free-stock shelter. This wing was simply a huge open area with a door leading to the lot and a long feed bunker down the center.

"Hey, Dad," Jon said suddenly, "you forgot a stall for Sunny. What about him?"

Dad's blunt, black-rimmed fingernail jabbed the blueprint in the center of the stock shelter area. "That's twenty-two by forty feet. Your damn horse will have the biggest stall in the country, and he'll have it all to himself after the cattle are sold this fall. I don't want to hear any more about that poor underprivileged horse now."

There was an edge to his voice. Jon flushed, and Elton glanced away from the television screen for an instant.

In the silence of the dining room, Dad began to look uncomfortable. He leaned over the blueprints, concentrating. The light fixture that hung low over the center of the table was just a few inches from the bare white top of his head. The pale skin contrasted more sharply than usual with the salt-and-pepper fringe of hair around it, and the Indian red of his lower face. Harsh shadows from the light accentuated the strength of the man's features, strength that was undiluted by the increasing thickness of his jowls, strength that Jon knew would never show on his own face.

Standing slightly behind Dad, seeing his profile above the familiar pale blue shirt and Oshkosh overalls, Jon felt a hating, envying, yearning, resentful love for this man who was his sire.

"Tell you what," Dad said. "This door here, from the cattle area to the lot. We might make that a Dutch door. Then in nice weather, you could leave the top part open when you shut the horse in there, and he could look out. How'd that be?" He didn't look up from the blueprint.

Jon came close to the table. He studied the plans for a longer time than necessary before he said, "That'd be a good idea, Dad."

Later that evening, while Dad was still in an approachable mood, Jon said, "Since I've got to get a new bridle anyway, and since the old army saddle got burned, do you suppose it'd be okay if I take what's left of last year's hog money and get me a good matching saddle outfit? Not a real expensive one, but good quality and nice enough for if I ever wanted to ride Sunny in some local shows and parades and stuff? I've still got a couple hundred dollars left."

Dad frowned, sighed, shifted in his chair. "I don't know. I hate to see you spend that money for a saddle, with school coming up and all. Tell you what. Why don't you hold off on the saddle till after you sell this year's pigs. They should be ready to go about late October, early November. You ought to be getting twelve or thirteen hundred dollars out of this batch. Put a thousand of it in your college fund, and I don't care what you do with the rest."

Jon let out his breath. "Right. It's a deal."

A few days later Sade came home from the clinic. A metal rocker on the bottom of her cast enabled her to walk fairly comfortably, although she made a heavy clumping sound on the bare floor. The torn front paw was nearly healed, and the singed coat had already begun to grow out. Except for the cast and a noticeable disinfectant smell about her, she seemed completely herself.

On the first night she was home, Jon made a bed of rag rugs for her in the kitchen, in the corner where her pen had been two years ago.

"There you go, Sadie. Now you won't have to climb those old stairs till your leg gets better. G'night, girl."

Before he was halfway up the stairs, she was behind him, pulling herself awkwardly up one step at a time, dragging the cast loudly behind. In the bedroom, she began to struggle up onto the bed. Finally Jon boosted her.

"You big nut. You're bound and determined to sleep up there, aren't you?"

She stretched out with such obvious delight, thumping the blankets with her tail, that he shrugged and left her there. He skinned out of his clothes and settled onto the creaking bed diagonally. As he stretched his legs past the bulk of the dog, he smiled. It was kind of good to have old Sade back.

The end of summer came rapidly, and the fall work began. School began, too. Jon still rode the school bus and so had no time for after-school activities, evening football games, clubs, or committees. He was still an outsider, but he was seldom aware of it. The farm, Sun God, the work to be done—this was the real world. School was an interlude.

When the McBride hogs were marketed in the last week of October, they included nineteen of Jon's. Fortune, having twice fulfilled her duties as brood sow, was among them. The other eighteen were this spring's crop of male pigs borne by Fortune's five daughters. From these five litters, Jon again saved the females, twenty-three in all. Next year's crop of twenty-eight litters would make a healthy contribution to his college fund, even after he paid Dad for their feed.

This year, when Dad came home from the packing plant and did his figuring at the desk in the dining room, the check he wrote Jon was for thirteen hundred and twelve dollars and twenty-three cents.

That evening when his homework was done, Jon carefully tore the envelope out of the Sears catalog and made out the order blank. He had chosen the saddle weeks ago. The photograph of it was printed so clearly in his mind that he saw it when he closed his eyes at night. He could recite the description word for word.

"Western Cutter, Sears' finest! Black AA leather over rawhide tree, fifteen inch padded seat with Cheyenne roll. Fourteen inch swept-back front, sheep wool lined rounded skirt, leather-covered two and a half inch stirrups with quick-change buckles. Matching bridle and breastplate. One forty-nine ninety-five plus shipping."

He sealed and stamped the envelope and put it with his textbooks. As he went upstairs, he felt a growing sense of relief.

Only another week or ten days, he thought as he pulled off his sweater. Then no more riding with just the halter and rope reins, no more . . .

His mind turned uncomfortable from thinking about Sunny, about the spirit their rides were taking on, a subtle aura of combat that he refused to acknowledge consciously. There had been no open runaways recently, only a hint of arrogance about Sunny's head sometimes, a hesitation before he obeyed the pressure on his halter that told him to slow down, an exaggerated shying when there was nothing to shy at. It was as though he were showing Jon his contempt for the flimsy control of the halter, as though he were obeying because he chose to and not because he must.

It's all in my head, he told himself grimly. He's really behaving himself a lot better than he did at first.

And at least I'm a good enough rider now that I can stick with him when he shies. Still, I'll be glad to get a good old curb bit in his mouth again.

From the next room, he could hear Ernie talking, then laughing loudly into the ham radio mike. It reminded Jon of the night he'd overheard the twins' argument about Sunny.

"Too much horse for me to handle. Hah," he said. "I'll show 'em. Just wait till Elton comes home at Christmas, and I'm riding Sun God around in that black saddle outfit. That'll shut them up, won't it, Sadie?"

Her tail struck the bed.

16

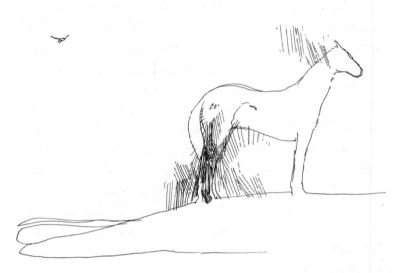

On the evening of November first, the contractor's workmen raked up their debris, patted Sade's head, and left. The barn was ready for use, although it still lacked paint and shingles and some finishing touches inside.

After supper, Jon and Ernie went out to admire it again, and to fix a place in the cattle shelter for Sun God. Freed from her cast, Sade followed the boys, circling their legs and urging them to go faster. In the last glow of sunset, the raw lumber of the barn turned from gold to soft pink. It stood out in lovely pastel against the quiet blue-gray of the cloudy twilight sky.

"It's a shame we can't paint it pink instead of white," Jon said. Ernie snorted.

Working together, they forked a generous pile of clean bright straw into one corner of the cattle shelter area. Jon filled and hung a water bucket, while Ernie climbed into the new haymow and threw down a bale of the hay Jon had bought last week from Cal White. They spread the hay in the feed bunker. Then Jon opened the Dutch door to the lot, and led Sunny in.

When he and Sun God entered, Sade was just finishing her third turnaround in the middle of the straw, and was curling down in its luxury.

"Hey, Sadie, no. Get out of there." Jon laughed as he scolded. "That's Sunny's bed. Move now." He let go of Sunny's halter and latched the bottom half of the door, leaving the top open to the crisp night.

Reluctantly Sade got up, stretched, shook off the straw in her coat, and relinquished the bed to Sun God. While Jon and Ernie watched, Sunny moved the length of the room, looking from side to side, extending his nostrils to the scent of the new wood, testing the feel of the place. He dipped his long head into the hay and gave it a stir. He tasted the water in the bucket that hung on the wall. He lipped over the oats and rock salt in the feed tray at the end of the bunker. When the oats were gone, he went to the corner where the straw was piled, stirred through it, pawed it into a heap in the center, and finally hung his head and dropped one hip. Jon went to him and

146

patted him good-night. Then he and Ernie, with Sade between them, trudged back to the house.

The next morning when he opened the door to the cattle shelter, he found it empty. The bottom half of the Dutch door showed double splintered nicks in its top side, where Sun God's hooves had failed to clear it completely. Far out in the pasture, beyond the two closed gates of the lane, a golden shape browsed among the sumac bushes.

As he stared at the distant horse, Jon realized that his feelings were hurt, childishly, by the obvious fact that Sunny preferred his freedom to the comforts his owner had provided. Mixed with the hurt was irritation at the impudent ease of Sunny's escape.

"Okay for you," he muttered. "Just stay out there. See if I care."

Indian summer came on Saturday morning. Most of the trees in the pasture and around the house had already shed their leaves, but a few deep red oaks and softer sumac bushes, and an occasional yellow maple, saved the farm from the gray-brown drabness that was on its way. The fields were stripped now, but there was enough left of stalks and stubble and empty plants to turn the landscape into a patchwork of muted rust and tan and brown-black. Mists lay in the low places, and although the morning was unusually warm, the sky was clouded to a soft, even gray-blue.

The fragrance of burning leaves came from some-where. Jon took the roofing nails out of his mouth for a moment, so their metallic taste wouldn't inter-fere with his enjoyment of the smell of the leaves. He was on the barn roof with Ernie, on the low part over the cattle shelter area.

They worked in easy silence, lining up the shingles, tacking them in place, making sure they were tight and even. He could feel the gravelly roughness of the new shingles through the knees of his Levis. Ernie began whistling something quietly through his teeth, and unconsciously Jon picked up the tune.

On the ground below them, Sade lay gazing out toward the pasture. The calves had been sold three weeks ago, but she still watched for them. One of the half-grown kittens who had survived the barn fire crept through the long grass near Sade's head, crouched, lashed its small tail back and forth, and finally leaped at her ear. Sade batted it away once, and then again. She growled a warning. The kitten backed off a step, thought it over, then circled Sade's head and curled down for a nap against the dog's throat. Sade sighed and went to sleep, too.

A little later Aunt Jess peered up at Jon over the low edge of the roof. "Jon, Railway Express just called. Your saddle's there. You can pick it up any time."

He dropped his hammer and started down toward her, but she stopped him. "You don't have time to go clear in to town now, though. I'm going to call lunch in a half hour or so."

He picked up his hammer.

"I'll take you in after we eat, if you want," Ernie said.

"Oh good. I think I'll just finish this row here, and then go catch Sunny and put him in the barn so I can try the new stuff on him as soon as we get back." The tempo of his hammering quickened.

"Hah. You think you can catch that horse and have him back here before lunch? What an optimist."

"Oh, he's not hard to catch. I bet you I can."

"Okay, buddy, put your money where your mouth is. How much?"

Jon forced his hand into his Levis pocket and came up with two dimes, a nickel, and a mixture of pocket lint and oat chaff. "Two bits says I'm back here, inside the lot, before she calls lunch."

They crawled toward each other until they met in the center of the roof. Jon slapped down his change beside Ernie's quarter.

"I hate to take money from a kid." Ernie grinned. He went back to work, whistling, while Jon skinned down the roof and dropped to the ground. He got the twine-braided reins and two ears of corn from inside the barn, then started down the lane at a fast lope.

Luck was on his side. Sun God was near the pasture gate, grazing on the frost-deadened meadow grass. When he caught sight of Jon, he raised his head. At that moment, the sun broke through. It seemed to point a narrow finger of light directly down on the horse.

Jon stopped. For an instant, he ceased breathing.

The horse was a painting Somber hillocks of grass, shadowed timber, bright gray-blue sky, all went out of focus. The beam of sun that took the form of a horse when it touched the ground—that was all he could see. The animal stood, head high, legs square beneath him, tail blowing forward around his hocks, mane a frothy profusion on the proud neck. The great dark eyes burned into Jon's heart

Then the sun was gone and the moment with it. Sun God lowered his head slightly, shook his mane, walked slowly toward Jon. He accepted first one ear of corn and then the other. The long, powerful jaws bore down on the corn, breaking off the kernels with a loud, hollow crunch. Nodding his head, Sun God dropped the second cob to the ground and searched the front of Jon's shirt for more.

With a sudden overwhelming wave of frustration, Jon wrapped his arms around the horse's neck and held on hard. He wanted to get closer, to reach inside the golden animal and pull—something out— to *force* Sun God to respond. He wanted to claw away the aloofness. He wanted to cry, to hit Sunny. . . .

Instead, he snapped the twine reins onto the halter and tossed the loop over Sunny's head. Stepping on

150

the edge of the salt-block stand, he threw himself up onto the high back and reined Sunny toward the barn.

Before Sun God bolted, halfway to the barn, Jon knew it was going to happen. Instead of fighting for control, this time he leaned forward into the whipping mane. Between his knees, he felt the muscled barrel extend itself, flatten itself. The wind sang against his face, drying his eyeballs.

Ahead loomed the barn. He braced himself for the stop inside the lot. It would have to be abrupt. He caught a glimpse of Ernie watching from the roof. There was a shout, but the wind carried the words away.

As they pounded into the lot, sudden terror washed over him. The barn tilted toward him. The bottom of the door was shut, but the top was open— a black square, incredibly small.

The terror left him, and he felt only betrayal. He screamed, "Sunny, please."

The square of black flew at his head, and exploded.

17

As the ambulance turned from the lane onto the road toward town, its siren moaned, then wailed. The sound of it shook Ernie from his stupor. He became aware that Cal White was standing beside him, and that Sade was whining at the barn door behind his legs. He opened the door for Sade, then turned to answer Cal's repeated questions.

"I don't know, Cal. He must have a fractured skull at least. It was bleeding something awful across . . ." His voice wandered as his mind rejected the memory.

"But what *happened*, Ernie?"

"Horse ran away with him again. Jumped the

bottom part of the door, trying to get into the barn. Knocked him off. He was—"

A scream shattered the air. From inside the barn came furious shuffling, a thin nerve-tearing wail.

Cal's and Ernie's eyes met for a split instant before the two men bolted into the barn. In the dim cave of the cattle shelter, Sun God was spinning, squealing, rearing away from a white devil that tore at his throat, that fell, leaped, sobbed.

Cal lunged for the flailing rope reins. He dodged Sun God's hooves and threw his weight against the horse's head, twisting it aside. Ernie dove for Sade, burying his fists in her back, her ruff, wherever he could, and hauling her back.

A hoof flashed past his face, fanning him with its breeze, as he rolled backward in the straw. Grimly he stumbled to his feet, arms locked around the shaking, bleeding, half-crazed dog. When her fury began to subside, he carried her into the other part of the barn, stumbling, his vision blurred.

"I don't blame you, Sadie," he mumbled into her neck. "I don't blame you."

Cal followed him out of the barn. When Ernie had shut Sade in the house, he said, "Do you want to ride in to the hospital with me, Cal?"

"I'd like to. Thanks. Listen, Ernie, I think it might be a good idea if I take the horse over to my place for the time being. Your dad is pretty worked up right now, and if—things—don't look too good at the hospital—with Jonnie—I wouldn't be too surprised at anything he might do to the horse when he got back."

Ernie nodded, and Cal went on. "I've got to go over home anyway. I think I left the motor running on the corn picker when I saw the ambulance. I'll just take Sun God on over now, and you can follow in the car, okay?"

Again Ernie nodded. He went to the house to get the car keys and, coming out again, paused on the back steps to watch Cal leading Sunny down the lane. The horse was favoring one front leg, but moved calmly. At the mailbox, he dipped his head to snatch at a clump of grass. Ernie turned and bolted back into the house, for the bathroom.

Jon opened his eyes and found himself floating near the ceiling of a small tan room, or perhaps it was a large tan box. He didn't know who or where he was, and the questions were unimportant to him. A large yellow horse floated near him. When it wavered too close, he tried to raise his arm to protect his face. But the arm wouldn't move. Someone screamed.

Through a door that was only half a door, only a small black square in the wall, an angel or a nun floated toward him. She leered down at him, then spun away through an incredibly long, deep whirlpool that sucked away the room and the yellow horse and left him in blackness.

Much later, he was standing beside Sun God in the narrow stall in the old barn. He tried to raise his arm to curry Sunny's flanks, but the horse was crowding him, crushing his ribs into the wall of the stall. He couldn't breathe or cry out, and he needed to call someone, because the barn was on fire.

Then he was outside the burning structure, and Sunny was inside, kicking at the door and screaming. Jon pushed through the heavy air, reached for the door, clawed at it. The door opened, but one of his fingers had torn off on the door latch. As he fell to the ground, Sun God leaped out, trampling him.

The tan room wavered into his dream, and someone was crushing his ribs the way Sun God had done in the stall. Only this was a man. There were loud voices in the background, Aunt Jess's and some others, but they were talking in a foreign language. It irritated him. He tried to speak, to tell them to talk softer and to use English, but then they all drifted away and left him standing beside the mailbox.

He was very small, or else the mailbox had grown to gigantic proportions, because the top of his head was lower than the red metal flag on the side of the box. As he stood there, Margie White came by, riding a mammoth golden horse. When she stopped beside him, he noticed that there was a sunbeam following them, spotlighting the horse, turning it into something that belonged to the sky. The horse looked down at him with soft and loving brown eyes, but his ears were flattened against his head, and the red lining showed in his nostrils.

"You can't ride him," Margie taunted. "You're too little. He's no kid's horse."

He tried to call after her as she galloped away, to warn her about the horse, but his chest hurt too much.

The time finally came when he was awake, and knew he was awake. Although he felt no desire to open his eyes, he knew who he was, that he was in a room at the hospital, and that the voices he heard were Dad's and Cal White's. He knew, without remembering when he was told, that he had a concussion and some broken ribs. With his eyes still closed, he concentrated on the voices.

". . . horse is a killer, Cal, and I'm not going to take any more chances with him. He's going to be destroyed, and that's that. I appreciate your taking care of him all this time, and I'll see you're not out anything for the feed and all."

Cal's voice was low. Jon had to strain to hear it.

"John, I been a horseman all my life, and I've been watching this horse every day for two weeks now. Believe me, he's not a killer or anything like it. He's a lot of horse, and Jonnie hadn't done much riding before he bought him. The animal knew he could take advantage, so he did. Jon shouldn't ever have trusted him like he did, riding him with just a halter and lead ropes, but what happened was an accident,

John. You can't have the animal destroyed just because Jonnie trusted him too far."

Dad started to answer, but Aunt Jess's voice cut
in. "If you two will stop and think for a minute, you'll
realize it's not your decision to make. That horse is
Jon's property. Cal, you might be right. I have a lot
of respect for your judgment, and you're in a position
to be fairer about it than we are.

"I'm inclined to agree with John right now. but
that's neither here nor there. The fact is Jonnie's got
to be the one to make the decision. Stop and think,
John. If you have that horse destroyed, and don't give
the boy any say-so in the matter, he'll never get over
it, and he'll never forgive you."

Jon lay in the sudden silence of the room and felt
the tears push out between his tightly closed lids and
slide down his face toward the pillow.

He was wide awake and fully conscious during
the ride home in the back of the now-silent ambulance. The ambulance drivers carried him up the narrow stairway and settled him in his own bed. It was
unbelievably wide and soft and low and dear. Sunlight poured in the east and south windows and
touched the dresser at the foot of the bed. Aunt Jess
had put a vase there, with an artless but colorful arrangement of sumac and ryegrass and beautiful-ugly
milkweeds.

She stood near the bed, holding firmly to Sade's

collar. The twins were there, grinning awkwardly down at him. Dad moved uncomfortably from window to window, as though he would rather be outside. They talked stiffly, saying nothing.

Finally Jon said, "Is Sunny still over at Cal's?"

An air of tension filled the room. Dad nodded, still looking out the window.

Jon waited for someone to say something, to start things and get it over with. No one did. He didn't want to ask, but he couldn't stand not to, so he said, "Well, when can he come home?"

Dad turned toward him, opened his mouth, then glanced toward Aunt Jess. The twins melted back away from the bed.

Aunt Jess came close and looked down at him. He cringed away from the loving concern on her face. "Jonnie, you've got to make a decision about Sun God. You realize that, don't you?"

Jon braced himself. Here it comes, he thought. This is it. But I *can't*—not Sunny. . . .

Slowly, evading her eyes, he nodded.

Dad cleared his throat. "Now, Son, personally I don't want that animal on the place again, but he's your horse, and the decision is yours. If you've got the sense I think you have, you'll do the wise thing."

Jon turned his face toward the wall.

"Hey, buddy," Ernie said brightly, "who was that guy that was here, remember, last summer? He

158

made you a good offer for Sunny, didn't he? Why don't you get hold of him?"

Through the bitterness that burned inside him, some part of Jon recognized, and bowed to, Ernie's logic. "I threw away his card, and I don't remember his name," he growled.

"He was from Boone or Marshalltown or some-place around there, wasn't he? And didn't he have a car agency of some kind?" Ernie's cheer lifted a little of the tension in the room. "I know what I'll get on the old ham set and call everybody I know around Boone and Marshalltown. Somebody's bound to know the guy." He escaped to his own room, with Elton close behind.

Dad took a deep, relieved breath, as though the whole thing were settled. "Tell you what. If you sell this horse, and if you feel like it later on, maybe you can buy another one that's a little gentler. Now, doesn't that sound like the sensible thing to do?"

Jon closed his eyes and saw Sun God looking down at him through the dimness of the sale barn stall; Sun God silhouetted against the green of the pasture and the brilliant summer sky; Sun God thundering across the grass, racing the phlegmatic calves; Sun God posing in the beam of sunlight, his mane and tail a froth on the wind.

Slowly, wearily, he nodded.

Through the aching misery that expanded inside

him, he was aware that Sade's head was on the bed, boring under his arm, striving toward his face. "Hi, Sade, old girl," he whispered.

In an instant, she was beside his head, her front paws on his taped chest, her muzzle thrust between his neck and the pillow. Her tail whirled furiously as one back leg sought a foothold on the edge of the bed.

His arms locked around her neck. "Hey there, Sadie. Did you miss me while I was gone?"

#2468